MW00479769

DANCING IN
THE DARK

AN FBI KNITTING GAME MYSTERY SPINOFF – BOOK 1

HILARY LATIMER

Copyright © 2019 by Hilary Latimer

All rights reserved.

No part of this book may be reproduced in any form or by any electronic or mechanical means, including information storage and retrieval systems, without written permission from the author, except for the use of brief quotations in critical reviews and certain other noncommercial uses permitted by copyright law.

Cover Art, Interior Layout & Proofing: Madeline Farlow at Clause & Effect

This e-book/book is a work of fiction. Names, characters, places and incidents are either products of the authors imagination or are used fictitiously. Any resemblance to any actual person, living or dead, events or locals is entirely coincidental.

The author acknowledges the trademark status and owners of the following trademarks mentioned in this work of fiction: Subaru, Ferrari, Lamborghini, Lincoln Town Car, Chevrolet, Buick, The Oscars, Oscar, The Golden Globes, Batman, The Kodak Theatre, The Nuart Theatre, The Staples Center, Botox, Taser, Smith & Wesson, Griffith Park Observatory, CalTech, UCLA, USC, Crock-Pot, Google, *Criminal Minds*, Little Shop of Horrors, Fibre Space, Glock, McDonalds, Ford, Uber

The fictional band *Broken Wings* and the lyrics of their songs are the creation of author T. K. Gardiner and are used with permission

The Special Investigations Unit of the FBI, the movie, *Entangled,* The Knitting Game and Criminal Knits are the creation of the author

The author acknowledges that the jurisdictional dividing line between West Hollywood and Beverly Hills has been altered to include a fictional parking lot for purposes of this story

Also available as an ebook.

CONTENTS

ONE
THE SECRET GARDEN

The garden was old. Abandoned. Overgrown. Spooky, even. The perfect place to dispose of a body. It would be months, he thought, before anyone even noticed the old woman was missing. Time enough for her bones to slough off their skin and muscle. A smile quirked his lips. He wondered if that Fed whose videos MurderDude kept posting online knew how useful his lectures were. How-to guides, practically, on the best ways to hide a body. Not what he'd intended, most likely, since it was some kind of bullshit psych class. He gave a snort of laughter. Oops. Well, not everyone could be as smart as he was. He smiled and looked around. Then, closing his eyes, inhaled deeply. The mingled scents of bitter blood and rotting wet leaves danced across his senses. While a note of wild rose wove itself around them. A requiem, so to speak, for the dead woman at his feet.

Out past the tangle of trees and overgrown bushes, he could hear the sound of an engine idling: Dad waiting patiently for him. He knew there was no need to hurry—the car had a full tank—but he didn't feel the need to linger, or bury her. Like those guys who had to hide what they'd done. Dead was dead. It was the dying that was interesting, and he wasn't a freaking undertaker.

Brushing his hands off on his thighs, he stood slowly, stretched, then began to pick his way out of the clump of trees back toward the driveway, his stomach growling in counterpoint to the throb of the engine. Time to feed a different hunger, then.

He thought about the possibilities for dinner. Fried chicken sounded good, with green beans and mashed potatoes, maybe? And gravy. Definitely gravy. As he pondered what he'd like for dessert, he slipped a tarnished house key into his pocket. It was old fashioned, heavy, a nice addition to his collection.

All in all, it had been a very good day, and oh! a nice peach cobbler would be the perfect way to end it.

Special Agent Fountain Rhodes had a headache. The kind that made him want to squeeze his brains out through his eyeballs. It happened every time he had to teach. The headaches crept in slowly on tiny, cat-like feet, kneading their claws into every nook and cranny of his skull until he wanted to scream. Those were the kinds of headaches he got in the mornings.

The ones he got in the afternoons were the kind only a bullet through the temple could relieve. And yet they still made him teach, even though he was terrible at it, because he could "connect" with the students better than most of the other agents could—meaning he didn't look like a slab of beef and he lost his place and tended to go off on wild tangents and . . . he was completely nonthreatening, with a capitol N and a capitol T. One of the many reasons the Bureau loved him. He wasn't entirely sure he loved *it* right now, but at least he had the next hour free to get rid of his current headache before he got another one during his afternoon seminar. It wasn't even that he hated teaching—at least not at Quantico where no one cared if he slid off topic as something new about an old case caught his attention—but when he was guest lecturing at one of the universities in the D.C. area, like now, he was supposed to stick to the subject at hand. Something he wasn't very good at.

Stepping off the path he'd been following through the hustle and bustle of campus, Fountain made his way into the small, secluded garden where he intended to spend his lunch hour. The cool dark shadows thrown by the towering sycamore trees were a balm to his soul. The perfect place to find some peace and quiet. Or to bury a body.

The thought came unbidden, and he found himself looking around for signs of disturbed ground or freshly dug telltale mounds. Then with a muffled snort, he shook his head. He was being ridiculous. There weren't any bodies buried here. God, he needed a life outside of work if he was imagining crime scenes now where there weren't any. A hobby, a girlfriend, a pet —something.

A girlfriend would be nice, but most of his dates pretty

much ended about the time they started pumping him for the grisly details on whatever case he was working. Law enforcement groupies. By now he should have been able to spot them a mile away. But no. He still got blindsided when they put a hand on his thigh, batted their eyelashes and said, "So tell me about the case you're working on right now. I won't tell a soul. Promise."

Why was meeting someone who was interested in *him* so damn hard? With a weary sigh, he reached into his satchel and fished out a small, leather-bound book. Setting the bag on the ground he collapsed in an ungainly heap beside it, gave his shoulders one last tension-relieving roll, then leaned back against the rough bark of the sycamore tree, whose shadows he intended to hide under until he had to teach again and began to read.

The small garden Rhodes was in was old and overgrown with a deep border of shrubs and flowers. Wrought iron tables and chairs waited silently in the center for someone to use them, while towering oaks and sycamores stood thick against the old brick walls, sentinels watching over the place.

Leaves skittered on the ancient brick walkways as the stuttering breeze picked them up and tossed them. Small birds flitted from bush to ground and back again, sharing their joy at the warm sunny day with peeps and whistles, happy for one last taste of summer, while the squirrels and chipmunks went back about their business, done with scolding the lanky intruder who had invaded their space.

Content in the knowledge the denizens of the garden would warn him if anyone approached their domain, he lost himself in the rhythm of the words as the garden rustled and sighed around him. Small familiar sounds that soothed the tension of the morning away.

He felt the beat of the garden shift as the birds and squirrels stilled, leaving only the faint rustle of leaves in the tree tops as a breeze drifted through them. Seconds later he heard it—the slapping sound of feet running on the old brick walkway. He looked up, annoyed at having his peace and quiet disturbed, until he caught sight of the owner of the feet. His heart went thump, because simply put, he thought she was the most beautiful woman he'd ever seen.

Long dark brown hair streamed out behind her as she ran, a mischievous smile curving her full pink lips as if she had a secret she hadn't shared with anyone yet. She was deeply tanned from the long hot summer, the golden brown of her skin a sharp contrast to the white T-shirt she'd pulled up and knotted off to the side at her waist. Equally tanned legs flashed from beneath a short, ruffled, tie-dyed skirt, all bright greens and turquoise blues in a burst of heady color, while her bare feet had been shoved into old-fashioned scuffed white tennis shoes. Fountain was relatively certain he'd just fallen in love.

Catching sight of the little seating area in the center of the garden, the woman's grin widened in delight. With a joyful laugh, she skipped toward it, spun around once, then with arms outstretched, flung herself down onto one of the chairs. Tipping her head back toward the sun, she closed her eyes and gave a contented sigh, completely unaware of the awestruck man hidden in the sycamore's shadow.

And he was. Very awestruck. Because up until now Fountain hadn't believed in love at first sight—quite possibly because the closest he'd ever gotten to it before was falling in lust. But he thought he could very easily fall in love with this lovely woman given half a chance. A lovely woman who had no idea that he was tucked away in the shadows, he realized with a start.

He'd just opened his mouth to say, "Um, hi?" when a voice outside the tall brick garden walls suddenly bellowed, "Molly? Molly, where the hell are you?"

The young woman clapped her hands over her ears, but she was still smiling. Something Fountain also found himself doing, because her name suited her perfectly.

"Molly!" the voice cut off abruptly as a small, slender woman wearing a severely cut, dark blue suit strode into view. She had short, wildly curly red hair, low-heeled no-nonsense shoes, and, judging by the scowl on her face, she was plainly furious. "There you are! Martin's been looking everywhere for you!"

"Well, good for him," Molly murmured under her breath, completely unimpressed with the woman's pronouncement, although a smile still danced on her lips.

Clearly having heard her, the redhead snapped, "He wanted to have lunch with you!"

Molly tilted her head to the side and said, "Well, maybe I didn't want to have lunch with him. Did you ever think of that, Ricki?"

And Fountain thought, Ricki? Even as his mind began to race through the possibilities. Rick, Eric, Erica—ah . . .

The redhead, Ricki, huffed out a breath and said, "You're being ridiculous. The two of you would be perfect together."

"Except for the fact I can't stand him," Molly pointed out dryly, rolling her eyes.

"What's not to stand? He's tall, built, and handsome!"

"And vain and pompous and a conceited jerk. If you like him so much, why don't you have lunch with him?"

Ricki threw up her hands before placing them on her hips, then, glaring at Molly, said, "So what, Molly? You're going to spend your lunch hour here alone in this awful, smelly place, instead?"

"Ricki, it's a garden! It's neither awful nor smelly, and yes, I am."

"Really? Did you even think about the fact that something could happen to you while you're hiding here?" Ricki snapped. "You could be kidnapped or murdered or raped!"

"Could you get any more melodramatic?" Molly asked, at the same time as Fountain said.

"I wouldn't have let anything happen to her." He couldn't help himself—the words just slipped out.

Both women gasped, their eyes probing the shadows for whoever was hidden there.

He unfolded himself slowly and stepped into view.

"What, *you?*" Ricki scoffed, catching sight of him first.

Fountain sighed. He was used to it. He knew he was no one's idea of what a hero looked like. Tall and lean, he looked more like a hip college professor than a federal agent. Another reason the Bureau loved him and let him wear his hair a little longer than he should have, and turned a blind eye to his sports coats and two-toned winged tipped shoes when he was teaching— much to his bosses' chagrin, but with the assistant director's blessing.

"I'm with the FBI," he told her. "I wouldn't have let anything happen to your friend?" It came out more of a question than he had intended.

"The FBI?" Ricki echoed, her tone of voice quite clearly saying "*really?*"

He reached into his jacket pocket and pulled out his credentials, holding them up for her inspection.

"Huh—so you really are a Fed," she said grudgingly. "The gun-carrying kind?" she added after giving him the once over again, clearly still trying to reconcile his looks with her image of what a Fed should look like.

He pulled back his jacket to reveal the standard issue Glock under his arm.

"There, you see!" Molly laughed. "I was perfectly safe! And

if Agent—" She paused, looking up at him through eyes as brilliantly blue as the waters of the Caribbean.

For a minute, Fountain's breath caught in his throat as he tumbled head over heels into them. "Uh, Rhodes. Fountain Rhodes." He mumbled, still caught in their depths before wrenching himself free of their spell. "Though it's Special Agent, not Agent," he added quickly, because people always got it wrong, and for some reason he didn't quite understand, it was important that she knew that.

She smiled, those blue, blue eyes lighting up and suddenly, butterflies were dancing in his stomach.

"Well, if Special Agent Rhodes will stay here a little longer to protect me, I can finish my lunch break knowing I'm safe and sound."

"I'd be glad to," he agreed quickly, then blushed. God, could he sound any more like a fifteen-year-old with his first crush?

The woman, Ricki, gave him a cold stare, then turned to her charge? Rhodes wasn't sure what their relationship was, exactly.

"Fine then, fifteen minutes!" she snapped, not in the least bit happy about it.

"Twenty-five," Molly countered gently, before adding, "Goodbye, Ricki!" Then, leaning her head back, she closed her eyes and pretended to sunbathe again until the telltale click of heels faded away into the distance.

"She's gone," Rhodes said finally.

Sitting up, the young woman sighed. "She's a bit of a terrier sometimes," she confided. Followed by, "Wow! A real live FBI agent!"

Rhodes frowned slightly, confused. Did she know a dead one?

With a little giggle, she added, "God, you scared me. I didn't know you were there!"

"I was reading," he held up his book.

"And it was peaceful and quiet until I came along."

"Yes. No!" *Shit.* "It doesn't matter. I mean, I've read it before." He broke off, flustered. *Damn it!* Then, taking a deep breath, he tried again. "Um, your friend? She's very possessive of you." Great, now he was profiling. But the young woman just nodded her head in agreement.

"It's her job, I suppose. She's my manager." She shrugged, raising her delicate shoulders.

Her what? He raised his eyebrows at a complete loss.

"We're filming a movie over there," she explained, waving a hand toward the direction both she and Ricki had entered the garden from. "She's just doing her job, keeping track of me."

"Oh." He licked his bottom lip, wishing he knew how to keep her talking. She had the most beautiful husky voice.

"So, Special Agent Rhodes," she said drawing her legs up under her, "what brings *you* here?" Her eyes were alive with curiosity and—something more?

He swallowed hard, the first tendril of panic licking at him the way it always did when someone he was attracted to asked him questions. Which was stupid, but he was always a mess until they got past the realization that he was a little different—and were okay with it. Just breathe, he told himself.

"Um. I'm guest lecturing . . . and you don't have to call me Special Agent. Rhodes is fine. Or Doctor Rhodes , I suppose, though no one really calls me that. So, yeah. Rhodes is fine."

She laughed. "Well, Rhodes," she breathed his name silkily, "it's nice to meet you. I'm Molly Whittier." And tilting her head, she looked deep into his eyes as if expecting some kind of reaction, and not of the sweaty palm or wildly beating heart variety.

The quiet of the garden stretched out around them for just a heartbeat too long, as if the man was searching for the correct response before blurting out, "Nice to meet you too, Molly." Then he blushed and ducked his head, obviously embarrassed at his own awkwardness, which Molly found charming and endearing and . . . Oh god, the man was attractive, and he didn't even know it, she mused. Tall and broad shouldered with the lean build of a runner, he took her breath away.

He was beautiful, too—almost pretty with gorgeous chocolate-brown eyes and the longest lashes she'd ever seen. His copper-streaked, dark brown hair was longer than she thought a Federal Agent's would be, falling in untamed messy curls along the back of his neck. But for all the pretty angles and planes of his face, the hint of shadow along his jaw was pure, breathtakingly, male.

"So, what does an FBI agent read?" she asked, wanting to keep him talking.

"Um. Poetry?"

She couldn't help grinning. She loved the hesitant way he talked, turning everything he said into a question. He couldn't be that insecure really, could he?

"Wow—heavy stuff!" she teased. It took him a moment to get it, and he blushed again.

She tilted her head and looked at him, really looked at him. There was something a little different about this man. Something she found very appealing, despite of, or maybe in addition to, the slightly confused clothes he was wearing.

He had on a dark gray tweed jacket over a pale pink shirt with the top button undone. His charcoal-gray corduroy pants, while eccentric, at least went with everything else. But it was the rest of what he was wearing that thoroughly charmed her. His tie, which had been tugged down and pulled slightly off center, was inexplicably blue with a chestnut paisley pattern on it. A color scheme that was repeated in his blue and chestnut wing tipped shoes which, she was relatively certain, he had no idea didn't go with the rest of what he was wearing.

Or simply didn't care.

And she couldn't help it—she loved the way it was all just a little bit off-kilter, much like the man who was wearing it. He didn't look Federal Agency at all, which raised the question, why wasn't he dressed like a Federal Agent?

She raised an eyebrow and asked him. "How come you're not wearing your 'Men in Black' suit?"

He laughed, eyes crinkling up at the corners, plainly amused and delighted at her reference. "Ah well, I have special dispensation to not wear one when I teach. The Bureau doesn't want me scaring the kiddos and it also acts as a reminder that you don't need to be all muscles and scowls to be an agent, either. That they hire people from all different walks of life."

Which reminded her of something he'd said earlier. "So, what kind of doctor are you?" she asked curiously.

"The other kind," he answered automatically.

"The *other* kind?"

"Not the doctor, doctor, kind. Well, yes, I am, but—*damn*," he muttered, flustered again. "I'm a shrink."

She laughed. "I didn't think shrinks liked to be called shrinks."

He smiled back, "it doesn't bother me any. And it's not like I see people, professionally, so," he shrugged, "I'm good with it."

"You don't practice?"

"Nah. I pretty much have it down pat."

She snorted inelegantly, then giggled, loving his unexpected sense of humor and was rewarded with a shy smile of his own. Who knew a shrink could be funny, and sexy? And he was, very. "So, if you don't sit around all day asking people how they *feel* about things, what do you do at the FBI, exactly?"

"Sometimes I get asked to put on my shrink hat and listen in on interviews, and sometimes I get asked to conduct them."

"And when you're not wearing your shrink hat?" She prodded.

"Ah, then I wear my mathematician's hat."

"Your mathematician's hat?" She smiled at the image that came to mind of Rhodes wearing a tall pointy wizard's hat with mathematical symbols sketched on it.

"Yeah," he said smiling back. "I, um, I actually have a doctorate in Mathematics, too."

Wow. Gorgeous *and* smart, which, instead of being off putting, made him even more attractive. "So, you, what, combine the two together somehow?"

He nodded enthusiastically. "Yes, exactly! By combining mathematical principles with the principles of psychiatry, I can look for anomalies, patterns, things that aren't what they *should* be or aren't *where* they should be. Which, in turn, can help to determine patterns in behaviors. Like, the next possible step a serial killer might take, or the physical reality of tracking down where a white-collar criminal hid something."

No wonder she found him so appealing, Molly thought. Stupid men bored her silly and Special Agent Fountain Rhodes was anything but. In fact, he reminded her a lot of her brother, and suddenly everything about the man fell into place.

"You're brilliant, aren't you?" She asked, relatively sure what his answer would be.

Suddenly shy again, he licked his full lower lip, before nodding. "So they tell me," he said simply.

"Cool."

He blinked myopically at her, surprised, then laughed out loud before covering his mouth, embarrassed by his outburst. Then with a self-conscious grin said, "I'm not sure anyone's ever thought I was cool before."

"Oh, believe me, Special Agent Rhodes, you are *way* cool." And way too socially insecure for your own good, she added mentally. Or was it just because of her?

She tilted her head again, mulling that over. But no, she didn't think so. He hadn't reacted at all to her name. Which was a little ego busting and, a little refreshing, too. And interesting, now that she thought about it. Apparently, Special Agent Rhodes didn't watch many movies. She wondered what he did do when he wasn't working. Well, she knew of one thing.

"So, what kind of poetry were you reading?"

He blinked, his thoughts obviously elsewhere.

"Um . . . American, modern."

"Oh! That's my very favorite kind!"

Rhodes held out the little red leather book to her. "Then here, take it."

"Really?" She leaped up and skipped over to him, their fingertips brushing briefly as she took the little book. She wasn't prepared for the little zing that danced between them when they touched and judging by his little gasp, he'd felt it too.

For a moment, time stood still, as if the very earth itself were waiting for something to happen with bated breath, before the moment was gone forever, snatched away by a voice barking, "Rhodes!" as a tall, dark haired, military-looking man in an impeccably tailored charcoal gray suit strode into view, radiating authority. The man's eyebrows rose as he caught sight of them together, and self-consciously, Molly took a half step back, clasping the book of poetry tightly against her chest as if he might take it from her.

"Um, Page, this is Molly Whittier," he said, introducing them hastily. "Molly, this is Assistant Special Agent in Charge Thomas Page."

"Miss Whittier," Pages voice was polite but distant.

Molly stared at him for a second before blurting, "Please tell me you don't go through that," she waved her hands, "title thing *every* time you get introduced to someone, do you?"

Rhodes gave a little cough, his hand barely concealing the grin that danced across his lips.

"Yes," Page answered, matter-of-factly. "We do. Rhodes, you have five minutes. Don't be late," he added, looking back at Rhodes again.

Rhodes nodded.

"Miss Whittier, it was a pleasure meeting you," Page said, sounding like it was anything but.

For a moment, Molly stared after him as he walked away, before she shook her head. "And I thought Ricki was tough, but she has *nothing* on Assistant Special Agent in Charge Thomas Page. That guy is scary."

Rhodes laughed. "He really isn't that bad. He just hates the whole 'guest lecturing' thing. If it were up to him, he'd just let me get on with it on my own, which would be a real mess," he added quietly.

"That bad, huh?" she asked sympathetically.

"Yeah. I tend to get a little carried away when I'm talking. So someone has to come with me to keep me on the straight and narrow."

She could see him getting a little too impassioned. She wondered what the scary guy did to stop him.

"So, what *are* you lecturing on, anyway?"

Rhodes hesitated for a minute, his shoulders drooping just a little, as if her interest saddened him. "On how the placement of bodies can be used as an indicator to determine a perpetrator's feelings about his victims, more or less."

"Oh, yuck!"

He blinked, obviously surprised by her reaction. "Yeah, pretty much," he agreed. He seemed to hesitate for a moment before saying, "I . . . I'm sorry, but I really do have to go." Bending down, he picked up a satchel that had been lying in the shadows. Then with a small smile added, "It was nice meeting you, Molly Whittier."

"It was nice meeting you too. And I'll take good care of your book. I promise."

For a long minute, their eyes held before he turned and started to walk away.

"Rhodes?"

He turned back quickly.

"Will you be here tomorrow?" she asked, an idea forming. She wanted to see this shy, brilliant man again.

He nodded. "I'll be here all week. Well, not in the garden," he added blushing. "I'll be over there," he waved toward one of the old brick buildings.

"But you'll have the same lunch hour, right?"

"Um. Yeah. Twelve to one fifteen."

"Great!" she said happily. "Is there anything you don't like to eat?"

He cocked his head to the side, puzzled. "No, not really. Except, I'm not overly fond of anchovies."

She beamed at him. "Me either!"

"That's—good, I suppose?" He said, clearly bewildered.

"Yes, it is," she assured him. "And if I promise not to bring anything with anchovies in it, will you meet me here for lunch tomorrow?"

He blinked, clearly surprised, a blush feathering his cheeks.

"Just say, 'Yes, Molly,'" she told him.

"Yes, Molly," he replied dutifully. Then, "But won't, um, Ricki be annoyed about that? Or Martin?" He couldn't help adding with a lopsided grin.

"More than likely," she agreed with a laugh, as if the idea delighted her. "But my private life is just that, private, and mine to do with as I please. And what would please me is to have lunch with you tomorrow, Dr. Fountain Rhodes."

"Well, in that case," he said, a slow smile crossing his face, "I would love to have lunch with you tomorrow, Molly Whittier."

"Then it's a date!" And darting forward, Molly planted a quick peck on his cheek before spinning around and running off down the path she'd come in by, leaving a very startled Federal Agent in her wake.

Yes! she thought, grinning so widely she thought her cheeks might split. She had a date with a gorgeous man who didn't care one iota that she was a movie star—if he even knew it, which, somehow, she doubted.

It had been a very long time since anyone had been interested in her as just plain old Molly Whittier, and she had a feeling the lovely man was very interested.

Pausing briefly at the motor home, which was her current dressing room, to drop off the book of poems, Molly took a moment to read the title.

The World is New and Odd and Funny and Scary. I Think I Like It. By Alexander Rhodes. *Wait.* She opened the book and read the first page.

Poet laureate, Alexander Rhodes's latest book is filled with the whimsy we've grown to associate with his writings. This newest collection is his best yet. An ode to his first child, you'll smile, tear up, laugh, and cry as he discovers the world around him. Brilliant.

Closing the cover, she traced the image of a tree on the banks of a babbling brook stamped into the leather. Then opening the book again, she flipped to the dedication.

To my son, Fountain, who sees the world differently than the rest of us. A joy and an inspiration. I love you so much. Dad

Wow, she thought, as she set the book down. How beautiful,

just like the man it had been written for. She couldn't wait to read the poems his father had written for him. Alexander Rhodes. She shook her head, smiling in disbelief. He was one of her favorite poets, and she was having lunch with his son tomorrow! His very sexy son. And she couldn't quite help the happy little grin that danced across her lips as she closed the trailer door behind her.

TWO

DISCOVERIES

Strangling someone was hard and scary, and not in a good 'oh this is delicious' kind of a way. He'd thought it would be more intimate but it had been more intimidating—mostly because he hadn't realized how noisy it would be. All that flailing around and grunting. Someone could have heard, especially when the trash can got knocked over, clattering to the ground, then rolling away down the alley. Sounded like a nine-year-old banging around on their first drum set. All crash, bang, boom. Who still had metal trash cans, anyway?

He also hadn't realized how long it would take. Almost as long as making a frozen dinner in the microwave. Right on cue, his stomach grumbled at the thought of food. He'd been planning on eating out, savoring a nice dinner and a glass of red wine. But now he just wanted to go home, talk things over with Dad. Wash the evening off his skin. Not that he'd actually touched the guy. He'd worn thick work gloves and a motorcycle helmet, thank god, or he would have been all scratched up. Another thing he hadn't realized—the potential damage that could have been left on his hands and face. Ah, well, live and learn, right? And it wasn't like he had to do it again. Not like someone was holding a gun to his head.

Wait.

Now there was an idea. Hmmm. A gun. Yes, he kinda liked that idea. Maybe he'd give it a try? He shrugged. It had to be better than strangling someone. He'd think about it after his shower while he was eating. Speaking of which, what was he going to eat now his dinner plans had been ruined? He scrunched his eyebrows together, thinking. He was pretty sure there was still a chicken pot pie in the freezer and that Pinot Grigio he'd bought a few weeks ago would go with it nicely. His stomach rumbled again, demanding attention. Time to feed the other beast, then.

He looked down at the interestingly shaped key he'd taken off the dead guy. It had 'teeth' on both sides. Huh, he wondered what it had opened, then grinned. Whelp, he knew one thing for sure: it wasn't going to be opening anything ever again.

Fountain gave a contented sigh and leaned back in his chair. Molly had hit the nail on the head again when she'd suggested roast beef sandwiches for lunch today. The beef had been perfect too—rare and piled high on fresh baked rye, with horse-radish and mayo.

Usually, his lunch was something grabbed off a food truck,

or not at all, or a sandwich he brought from home if he remembered.

"That was delicious."

"Something tells me you're a bit of a foodie, Dr. Rhodes," she teased, gathering up the papers their sandwiches had come in.

He laughed. "I am not going to deny it," he agreed contentedly.

"So, are you secretly a gourmet chef with all kinds of interesting gadgets in your kitchen?" she teased.

"Sadly, no. I don't cook much, except on the weekends, since it's just me." He shrugged. "What about you?"

"Oh, I love to cook, but not that ridiculous stuff you get in fancy restaurants. Real food. You know, like burgers and pot roasts and mac and cheese."

"So, no fancy gadgets either, then?"

She laughed. "I'm pretty sure my kitchen in L.A. has one of everything, but I almost never get to cook when I'm there. Mostly, it's trendy restaurants with people I'd rather not be with —costars, producers, directors, whoever. And when I do get a moment to just chill out, I'm usually too tired to do much of anything. If I'm lucky, my housekeeper, Jonathan, takes pity on me and cooks up something, or my brother, Michael, does."

Fountain smiled. "So, your brother, he lives out there too, then?"

"Yeah. We share a house. There's not much point in both of us paying ridiculous mortgages. Especially since, when I don't have to be in L.A. or on a movie set, I hide out at my mom's in Front Royal. And she definitely has every gadget known to man," she added with a grin he found himself returning as an image of Molly with flour on her nose danced through his head.

While at the same time, he thought, hmmm, Front Royal. That wasn't far. Only about an hour or so away. Close enough to see her when she was home—if she wanted to see him, that was. And he couldn't help the little spark of hope that flared in his chest, because he liked the idea of that, of being with Molly for more than just a few lunch dates.

"Penny for your thoughts?" she asked, blue eyes bright and sparkling.

Not a chance, he thought. Or at least, not yet. He didn't even know how Molly really felt about him. He'd Googled her, right after Page had asked him if he knew who she was, which, of course, he hadn't. So maybe he was just a pleasant distraction in the middle of her day. Maybe this is what movie stars did when they were on set. Found someone who wasn't in the movies to spend a little time with.

And yet . . . it didn't feel that way. She'd found any number of excuses to touch him during their stolen lunches. A hand on his arm as she'd leaned forward to share something funny with him. Fingers lingering in his as she'd passed him a fork or a napkin. A slow sensual touch at the corner of his mouth as she'd brushed a crumb, real or imaginary, from his lips.

Or maybe that was just his imagination playing tricks.

Well, there was only one way to find out.

As casually as he could, he said, "I was wondering if you might like to have dinner with me in Alexandria tonight? There are some great places to eat, and it's old and historic, if you like that kind of thing. I mean, if you don't have anything else planned, that is." That last coming out in a rush and a tumble of nerves and excitement. Because what if she said "yes"?

Batting her eyelashes at him Molly grinned. "Why, Special Agent Rhodes, are you asking me out on a real date?" And his heart did a little flip flop from happiness at the smile on her face.

He pretended to think about it for a minute, tapping a finger against his lips to keep from laughing out loud at the sheer joy of knowing she was going to accept, until he couldn't hold back any longer and said, "Why yes, Miss Whittier. I am asking you out on a real date."

And there it was again, that little touch as she leaned forward and placed her hand on his arm. "In that case I—wait!" She sat bolt upright. "Are we talking Old Town?" she asked, excitedly.

"Yeah, I was actually," he agreed, wondering why that had her practically bouncing in her seat.

"Yes!" She fist pumped the air. "There's this yarn shop I've been dying to get to, and it's in Old Town too!"

Ah, now he got it. "Yeah, there is. Fibre Space."

She laughed delightedly. "How on earth do you know that?" Her eyes opened wide. "Wait, you knit?"

He shook his head and laughed. "Uh, no. But Mom does,

and she loves that shop, so she's always having me pick stuff up for her there."

"So, can we go? Please? It's open until eight tonight, I think."

"Is that a 'yes' to the date, then?" he countered.

"Yes! I would love to go on a date with you, Fountain Rhodes," she agreed quickly, beaming at him. "I can't think of any other way I'd rather spend a Friday night!"

"Except in a yarn shop, maybe?"

"Well, that too," she admitted, laughing.

"Story of my life," he said, biting back a grin of his own.

"Poor baby," she snickered, patting his knee. "I'll knit you a pair of socks. How's that?"

And Rhodes felt his heart go thump. "Ah, bribery. I like that in a woman. But kisses work just as well." *Oh shit. He had not just said that.*

"Well, in that case, Special Agent Rhodes, I shall give you a kiss *and* knit you a pair of socks," Molly told him, leaning forward to do just that, and Fountain's heart missed a beat as her lips brushed against his.

"Molly, you're late!" Ricki's voice sliced between them, and they both jerked back as if they'd been caught doing something they shouldn't have been.

"Why?" Molly whimpered, pressing her forehead to his. "Why does the universe hate us so much?" Which made Fountain laugh. That was the fifth time they'd been interrupted trying to kiss, not that he was counting.

"It doesn't," he reassured her, daring a quick kiss of his own and Ricki be damned. "It just has really bad timing. Or we do."

Molly huffed out a breath, muttering something he missed. Then, with a grin, she sat up suddenly, eyes gleaming, and Fountain thought, *uh oh,* he was starting to recognize that look. "Well, then it's time we fixed that! Hey, Ricki! Guess what? I'm going out with Rhodes tonight, and I don't want to hear any fuss about it."

"No," Ricki snapped, coming to an abrupt halt in front of them. Her short curls bounced as she shook her head vehemently. "It's not safe. Someone will recognize you, and the next thing you know—"

"Yes, I am. Didn't you hear the 'no fuss' bit?" Molly interrupted.

"Molly, you can't go out without a bodyguard, and I can't just magic one up because you want to go out with—him," she said, lip curling in obvious distaste.

"I don't need a bodyguard, Ricki. Because no one's going to bother me when I'm with Fountain. He's an FBI Agent, remember? And besides," she plowed on, "it's a blue jeans and T-shirt kind of date, not a getting all dolled-up kind of date. So, no one's even going to notice me."

Ricki bared her teeth, ready to launch into all the reasons why Molly wasn't going anyplace.

"Not to mention no one's going to believe a guy like me would be out with a movie star, right?" Fountain pointed out reasonably. "I mean, one look at me, and they'll know they were mistaken." Which naturally stopped Ricki dead in her tracks.

"Fine," she snarled, "go out. But just so we're clear on this," she added, glaring at Fountain, "it's *not* a date."

"Yes, Ricki, it is," Molly said firmly. "It's most definitely a date. The kind with kissing, even," she added wickedly, which made Fountain blush and Ricki throw up her hands.

"God, please, spare me the details," she snapped. "Fine. It's a date, and Mr. FBI man is going to keep you safe, or he'll be answering to me." Checking her phone quickly, she added, "and now you're really late. Let's go! Let's go!"

Grabbing up the bag they'd pushed their trash into, Molly gave an exaggerated sigh. Leaning in close, she kissed Fountain on the cheek and whispered, "Any time after six, I'll be ready and waiting. And did I mention I could really go for a great big burger and fries tonight?"

"McDonalds it is then," Fountain said, as solemnly as he could manage, which won him a little shove and a giggled, "Idiot."

Detective Avery Tolliver stood beside the body, staring down at it—him—as May LaGrange, the medical examiner, walked him through the murder.

"Petechial hemorrhaging consistent with strangulation, and

seeing as how there's bruising around the throat, that's how I'm calling it."

She had New Orleans in her voice, and a little voodoo in her dark brown eyes, and Tolliver had been trying not to fall in love with her for some time now. He'd sworn off love after his third wife, but he hadn't completely ruled out the possibility of asking May out sometime.

"Nothing under his nails, but that doesn't mean he didn't try to fight back," she continued. "And I'm thinking someone must have heard something, since that trash can over there"—she pointed down the alley—"looks like it came from here"—she pointed to a lighter mark on the asphalt behind her. "It would have made a lot of noise rolling about."

"Huh."

She gave him a look. Embarrassed, he rubbed the back of his neck. Okay, so not the most intelligent thing he could have said, but he was thinking things through, running scenarios that made the most sense.

"I'm thinking lover's quarrel. Something like that. Something someone was *angry* about." You didn't strangle someone for laughs.

"You'll figure it out," she said, standing up, patting his arm, just a hairsbreadth away from him. And not for the first time, he thought how well they'd fit together. She was a tiny little thing, and he was . . . not.

They drove to Old Town in Fountain's ancient Subaru, a car that Molly thought suited him perfectly, finding a place to park practically in front of the yarn shop.

"You're one of those people who always finds a space near wherever they're going, aren't you?" Molly teased.

"I invoke the parking gods," Fountain said, seriously, but his eyes were twinkling.

"The parking gods?"

He shook his head sadly. "Ah, no wonder you can't get a good space. You mock them. They don't take kindly to mocking."

"You're such a goof," Molly said, laughing.

Frowning, Fountain asked, "Is that a good or bad thing?"

Patting his arm, Molly said, "It's good thing, Rhodes, a very good thing."

"Okay then."

Giving him a quick kiss on the cheek, Molly bit back a smile. She'd noticed before how sometimes Fountain got confused by things people said, as if he wasn't quite sure what they'd meant. Sweet, brilliant, quirky man, she thought, as he opened her car door and helped her out, then tucked her hand into the crook of his arm as if it was the most natural thing in the world.

As natural as opening the door to the yarn shop and slipping a hand to the small of her back to usher her through it in front of him. She found herself smiling, it was such a Fountain thing to do.

"Shit. I'm sorry!" he apologized, suddenly, snatching his hand back, and for a moment, she was confused. Before she got it. He was afraid he'd overstepped his boundaries. But she loved his attentiveness. Loved the fact he actually *paid* attention to her. It was so refreshing after the rudeness she usually experienced from men barging in through doors ahead of her, then not even bothering to hold them open so she could go through them too.

"Don't be. I love the fact you're a gentleman." The smile that lit up his face made her heart skip a beat. God, he was gorgeous. She was leaning in to kiss his cheek when a voice called out, "Fountain, is that you? I have your mom's order here!"

"God can no one leave us alone?" she huffed, and when he snorted out a laugh, she started laughing too. Okay, so, yeah, a yarn shop probably wasn't the best place to get all romantical.

"Great," Fountain called back. "We're going to look around for a bit. See what else we can find."

"Oh, I didn't see you had a friend with you."

"Um, yeah, I do."

"Well, let me know if I can help you find anything!"

"Sock yarn?" Molly asked, throwing Fountain a sly grin.

"Right down the aisle in front of you. Both sides."

"Thank you!" Molly called back.

"I'll just go, um, over there," Fountain said, waving vaguely.

"I won't be long," she assured him.

"Take your time. It's a yarn shop. I know how these things go, so I came prepared. I have a book, and there are couches."

Oh my god, Molly thought, could he get any more prefect?

A little later, she thought the same thing again as she pushed away her plate, stuffed to the gills with the best burger she'd had in forever, loving the fact he'd listened and taken her somewhere she could satisfy her craving.

The restaurant itself had been perfect too. Just off the beaten track where a few people had done a double take, but no one had bothered her. She'd ordered a froufrou drink, and he'd had an IPA, and they'd talked about their day laughing over little things. Enjoying just being together, like an old married couple.

The thought stopped her dead in her tracks. But that was exactly what being with Fountain was like. As if they'd been friends forever. Friends hovering on the edge of becoming lovers, taking their first tentative steps to see how they might fit together. To see if they *could* fit together with the very different lives they led. As they stepped back outside and he wrapped his fingers around hers, she realized with a warm fuzzy feeling that that was exactly what she wanted. She wanted the chance to see if they could find a way to be together.

They took their time walking back to his car, looking in shop windows, their fingers twined together, laughing over some of the more outrageous things they saw as they offered to buy them for each other. When he leaned back against the passenger side door and drew her into his arms instead of opening it for her, some part of her brain shouted, *Yes!* exulting in the fact he was finally going to kiss her. Really kiss her. And then her brain stopped working as he slid his lips over hers.

"Get a room!" Someone shouted.

No. No, no, no! This was *not* happening. Not again, and Fountain huffed out a frustrated sound as he pulled away from her.

"Fine!" she snarled. "That's what we'll do, then. But we don't need to *get* a room, because I already have one in D.C." She heard Fountain's breath catch in his throat, then his eyes met hers, his eyes intense, searching.

"We don't need to get a room," he told her, carefully. "I have a house right here in Arlington."

For the barest instant, time stood still again, as if it were teetering on the brink of something huge as it waited for her answer.

Something that could change their lives forever. Desire burned in his eyes, desire and want and need and so much more. It took her breath away, made her weak at the knees, because she wanted this man as much as he wanted her.

"Perfect," she breathed against his lips, as she gave them a fleeting kiss. "Take me home, Fountain."

And he did.

THREE

MANNERS

He'd been polite. Very. Considering he hadn't wanted to meet her father in the first place. But, according to her, her dad had insisted. Wanted to get to know the man she was dating. Ugh. There was a nauseating word. Dating. It had too many connotations. Too many expectations. Ones he didn't share. But he'd gone along with it, more to shut her up than anything. So, he'd sat there, in their ostentatious living room, in their big house up on the hill, and had answered all her father's questions.

Where did he go to college? What was he studying? What was he planning to do once he graduated? On and on and on, prying and prodding at who he was and all for one purpose: to ascertain if he was good enough for the man's precious daughter. Who cared? He was only using her for the sex she so freely offered. It wasn't like he was planning on spending the rest of his life with her. God, there was a vomitous thought. Marriage. No, thank you. And the man had yapped on. About himself. About his precious daughter. About how much money he made. Blah, blah, blah.

It had been an easy enough decision to make to kill the whole lot of them. The dad, the girl, her simpering mother, and muscle-bound oaf of a brother. After all, his brand-new gun was in his backpack, ready, willing, and waiting. But not until after dinner. No point in passing up a free meal, and as it turned out, quite a delicious one. Roast beef with all the trimmings, savory and pleasantly rare. He hadn't really cared for the Yorkshire pudding, but now that he knew it wasn't really his thing, he never had to eat another one.

He'd waited until everyone was done eating, sitting around just talking, too stuffed to clear away anything yet or get up from the table. He'd excused himself, gone out into the hallway where his backpack was, retrieved the gun, slipped off the safety, gone back into the dining room and bang, bang, bang, bang until it was done. Once it was, he thought, well, that was easy.

Then he'd waited. For the sounds of neighbors calling out to each other. For someone to come to the door. For sirens. Something. But the night remained silent except for a few overeager nightingales.

And then he'd cleaned up after himself.

First, he'd gone into the kitchen and, using his shirt to open the cabinet door, had gotten some rubber gloves from under the sink. He'd removed all the glasses and dishes he'd used from the living and dining rooms and had washed them. Twice. And dried them thoroughly before putting them back where they belonged. He didn't bother wiping his fingerprints off the chair he'd sat in. After all, the police didn't have them on record so there was no point in wiping them away only to miss one. Who left a single fingerprint on a chair they'd sat in? He didn't move the chair either, since there was also an empty one next to the son.

When he was done, he stood in the hallway, thinking it through. The girl had opened the front door. He hadn't gone to the bathroom. Hadn't touched anything he hadn't already taken care of, besides the chairs in the dining and living rooms and there was no way of determining when exactly he'd sat in them. So . . . he was good to go.

He lifted the house key off the nail by the back door and almost laughed. Was that really a tiny diamond set into the head of it? Well at least it was in keeping with everything else about the family and house. You couldn't get much more pretentious than that.

He wore the rubber gloves out the door, since there was another, smaller pair, still damp from some earlier use, where he'd found the first. Peeling them off, he stuffed them into his backpack beside the gun. After all, there was no point in getting rid of them. They were still a perfectly good pair of rubber gloves. He paused for a minute in the back yard to get his bearings because, naturally, the girl had driven them in her cute little expensive car. God, it was going to be a long walk. He'd need a snack by the time he got home, burning up all that energy. Hmmmm, he had some leftover spring egg rolls from last night that ought to do nicely.

"Ready to go to dinner?" Martin Riley asked, strolling up to Molly and stopping directly in front of her as she closed the door to her trailer. His overly strong aftershave settled like a choking cloak around them.

"Yes, as a matter of fact I am," Molly agreed, trying to wave away the offending smell. "So, if you'll excuse me, Rhodes is waiting."

"Wha—what?" Riley spluttered, confusion marring his perfect leading-man features.

"Let me make this as simple as possible for you, Martin," Molly said, stepping around him. "You see the man in the car over there? That's who I'm having dinner with tonight, not you."

Riley's dark blue eyes widened slightly. "Do I know him? Who *is* he?"

"No, you don't. Not unless you happen to know any Federal Agents."

"What? You can't be serious." He spluttered, not only at the thought that he'd know a Federal Agent, but that she was also turning him down to go out with one.

The fact that he hadn't even bothered to either ask her out ahead of time or find out if she had other plans for the night had plainly never occurred to him. No, Mr. My Ego Is Too Big to Even Consider That had just assumed she'd drop everything for a chance to be seen with him.

"No? And why's that?"

"Because . . . because he's—nobody!"

"Really? How odd. And here I thought he was a lovely, gorgeous, smart man. Just the type of man, in fact, a woman like me would like to go out with. How silly of me."

Waving a hand, Riley brushed aside what she'd said as if it were meaningless. "Don't be ridiculous, Molly. You're a movie star. Movie stars don't go out with men like that. They go out with other movie stars," he asserted confidently.

"Oh, you mean, vain, self-centered, narcissistic idiots like yourself?"

Martin Riley blinked, a slight frown marring his perfectly chiseled face like he was having a hard time understanding what she'd just said. Which he probably was, she thought uncharitably, since he was a complete idiot.

Abandoning the effort entirely, Riley changed tack saying, "Are you really serious, Molly? You're willing to be seen out in— that?" He sneered, staring at Fountain's car in abject horror. "For god sakes, at least buy your little boy toy something decent to drive you around in."

Which is when Molly laughed. Only an ass like Riley would assume something like that.

"First off, Martin, he's not a boy toy. I know this is hard to understand, but he's a full-grown man with a real job who doesn't see me as an object to simply have on his arm to make him look desirable," she told him. "And secondly, it's a great car which doesn't yell, 'look at me, I'm a douchebag with more money than brains,' something you couldn't possibly understand with your Ferrari's and Lamborghini's cluttering your driveway. Any other asinine statements you wish to make? No? Good, because you've kept me waiting long enough, and I'm starving."

And before he could utter another word, she pushed him out of the way, got into Fountain's clunker and said, "I really, really dislike that man, intensely."

"I had no idea," Fountain said, pulling away, a small smile hovering on his lips. "Although I'm a little bit hurt you don't think I could pull off the whole boy-toy vibe."

For a heartbeat, she just stared at him, before she started giggling uncontrollably. "Yeah, that, so not happening," she snorted.

"So, um, at the risk of sounding like a complete idiot, who was that?" Fountain asked.

Molly slid him a look, before she laughed. "Oh god, I wish he'd heard you say that!"

"So, I'm guessing that was Martin Riley?" he said, sheepishly.

"In all his pompous glory."

To which Fountain simply answered, "Ah." Obviously not impressed.

Smiling to herself, Molly leaned her head back and felt the tension of the day seep away. "God, I need a break. From Martin, Ricki—this place."

Slipping his hand into hers, Fountain said, "How about a trip to the beach with me this weekend, then? My parents have a beach house I'm pretty sure no one's using. We can leave whenever you're done shooting Friday. I can take the time off— god knows I'm owed enough. I'll even cook for you," he added, a grin dancing across his lips. "The kitchen's stocked full of gadgets we can play with."

And this was why she was falling so hard for him, she thought. No hesitation. No, 'what about me's. Just, 'what can I do for you,' because he genuinely wanted to.

"I'd love that," she answered simply. A few days alone at the beach with Fountain? God, yes. A million times yes. She wanted every second she could get with the man. Wanted the memories to store away greedily for the time when they'd be apart.

"I've booked a table for lunch at The Hay-Adams," Riley announced the next morning, during their first break of the day.

"Oh? How nice for you," Molly told him. "I'm sure you'll enjoy being on display."

He frowned. "You'll be there too."

"No, Martin, I won't. Yet again, I already have plans for today, which you would have known if you'd bothered to ask me."

"What, with that policeman?" He scoffed.

"He's a Federal Agent," she corrected, taking a deep, calming breath so she didn't grind her teeth or slug him. "And who I see is none of your concern. You and I are not now, nor will we ever be, a 'thing,' so let me make this perfectly clear: You and I will never be having breakfast, lunch or dinner alone together. Ever. Got that?"

Riley had been waiting for Fountain near the tables and chairs in the little garden Fountain had started to think of as his and Molly's. "Just so you know, Molly's only amusing herself with you," he said, a small, not-altogether-pleasant smile, curving his lips. "Besides, you're not her type," he added, looking Fountain up and down pointedly.

Biting back a smile, Fountain schooled his face to show polite concern. "Oh? What is her type, then?" he queried, pretty sure already what Martin's response was going to be. He did not disappoint.

"Me," Riley intoned, puffing out his chest grandly.

Bullseye, Fountain thought, stifling an amused snort. "Good to know. Thanks."

"Why are you hanging around her anyway? Don't you have conspiracies to investigate or something?"

No, not that he knew of . . .

"Uh, no, I'm teaching actually."

Riley's lip curled up in disdain. "Teaching?" He sneered. "What?"

Fountain smiled. "A series of lectures on the ways serial killers dispose of their victims and the psychology behind their methodology."

Martin blinked.

"So, you're what, just parroting *Criminal Minds* or something?"

Seriously? Fountain plastered on another smile. "No, that would be the other way around actually."

Riley narrowed his eyes. "Yeah, well, Molly doesn't like brainy guys. She likes guys like me."

"God, what a day, and it's only lunch time!" Molly said, plonking down the picnic basket she'd brought with her and leaning in for a kiss.

"And it looks like it's not going to get better any time soon," Fountain told her apologetically. Turning to see what he was looking at, she huffed out an exasperated breath as Ricki came storming down the path towards them.

"Martin is seriously annoyed with you *again*, Molly," Ricki snapped, hands on her hips, glaring.

So, what was new? Molly thought, unpacking the picnic lunch she'd brought to share with Fountain in 'their' little garden. But what she said was, "That's funny, because I'm seriously annoyed with him too." But Ricki kept right on going as if she hadn't heard her.

"He was planning on having dinner with you last night, and you brushed him off!" she said incredulously.

"I had plans, which he would have known if he'd bothered asking me first." Molly answered, but Ricki was on a roll.

"And now you've stood him up for lunch *too?*" she exclaimed, as if Molly had clearly lost her marbles.

Taking a deep breath, Molly set down the container she'd been holding and turned to look her manager in the face. "Ricki, pay attention," she said as calmly as she could, when what she really wanted to do was yell. "I was never planning on having dinner with Martin last night, or lunch with him today, which explains why I'm here with Fountain. And just so you know, I will not be having either one of them with Martin any time in the future, either."

"Fountain!" Ricki snorted, ignoring the fact he was sitting right there. "You need to be spending time with Martin, not, not —*him!*" she snapped, finally acknowledging his existence with narrowed eyes and a flick of her fingers in his direction.

Molly counted to ten before saying, "Who I spend my time with is none of your business, Ricki. None. Now go away and stop interrupting my time with Fountain. There is not now, nor will there ever be, anything between me and Martin Riley, no matter how much you want there to be. I spend quite enough time with that odious man as it is, and I have no intention of spending one more second with him than I have to."

"I don't think she likes me very much," Fountain said with a giant sigh, as Ricki stormed away. "Although I could be wrong, I suppose. She was a little wishy washy about that," he added, which made Molly snort out a small inelegant laugh. God, she loved his sense of humor.

"It's not anything personal. She just wants there to be a 'thing' between me and Martin so the tabloids have something to gush over."

"That makes sense, I suppose. Better gossip mileage than you having a 'thing' with a Fed. Although I doubt she's ready to throw in the towel just yet. Especially since Martin still seems to be on board with it," he added wryly.

"Not my problem. Sooner or later they're both going to have to accept the fact that there's a you and me, and not a me and him."

She heard his breath catch before he asked, "And is there a you and me?" His beautiful brown eyes searching her face.

"Yes," she said simply, and a heartbeat later, he'd caught her up in his arms, and the kiss he gave her left no room for doubt as to how he felt about that, either.

───

"Detective Tolliver? We've got multiple homicide victims at a La Jolla Avenue residence. West Hollywood is asking for assistance."

Looking up, startled, his bushy brows pulling together, Tolliver said, "We have what?" He could not have heard that correctly.

Sergeant Alejandro Sullivan, Sully to pretty much everyone,

tugged on his ear lobe and shrugged. "That's what I'm being told. Four dead at the dinner table. Single gunshots to the head. No signs of forced entry. Nothing missing," he read off his notes.

Just. Great.

"Maid found them this morning," Sully went on. "None of the neighbors heard anything."

Of course not, Tolliver thought, tugging on his own earlobe, unconsciously mimicking Sully. No one ever hears anything. He let out a sigh and pushed back his chair. Four dead at the dinner table, single gunshots to the head, sounded like some kind of drug related execution. Just. Freaking. Wonderful.

"You get to drive," he said, tossing his keys to Sully. He could feel a headache coming on. The kind you got when the brass started breathing down your neck.

The only bright spot in his day was that he'd get to see May.

FOUR

"SO, WHO IS HE?"

Newspapers were interesting things, he thought, carefully opening up the one he'd just bought. Unlike the news on TV or whatever you got through your internet provider, newspapers screamed whatever they felt like at you in bold three-inch type, right across the front page, where you couldn't skip over it or tune it out. It was right there. In your face. In all its bold majesty.

Four dead in West Hollywood family slaughter

He couldn't help preening just a bit. I mean, how often did you garner a headline? Even if the cops had no idea who'd done it. There was speculation of course. Drug dealers. A cult—really? What, did they think the Manson Gang had been reincarnated? And of course, everyone's perennial favorite, an unknown serial killer, rampaging through West Hollywood.

Bing! Bing! Bing! We have a winner!

"So, who is he?"

"Who is who?" Molly countered, hiding a grin as she batted her eyelashes at her mom.

They were sitting in the little nest of chairs and couches at the end of the warm, homey kitchen she'd grown up in, catching up on all the things that never got said during their rushed phone calls when she was shooting a movie. Which, thankfully, was now over.

She'd had about all she could take of Martin Riley and his bumbling attempts to make them an "item" no matter how many times she'd told him it was never going to happen.

She was more than ready to spend her time off curled up at home, doing nothing at all. Except for seeing Fountain as often as possible and knitting "Dancing in the Dark," a new shawl pattern she'd just purchased.

Thank god he was only about an hour away. Just a straight shot down the mountain to townhouse, and giant oversized bed, and . . . She should not be thinking about that with her mom watching her. Especially since Allie Whittier had always been a bit of a mind reader when it came to her daughter.

Allie laughed. "I'm your mom, sweetie. Moms know when their kids are seeing somebody, so spill the beans already."

And Molly couldn't help grinning back into her mom's hazel green eyes. At fifty years old, Allie Whittier was still a stunning beauty. Widowed unexpectedly just a few years before, she still only had a few strands of gray in her auburn hair.

"Okay, yeah, I am seeing someone," Molly admitted. "His name is Fountain Rhodes. Dr. Fountain Rhodes," she added, slyly, knowing exactly what her mom would say to that.

"Oh my god, a doctor! You're seeing a *doctor!*" Allie squealed, right on cue.

"Yeah, I am. Just not *that* kind, Mom. He's a shrink."

"And how do you *feel* about that?" Allie teased, not missing a beat.

Molly rolled her eyes. "Ha, ha, ha, very funny. But honestly? I feel really, really happy. Oh, and did I mention he also has a PhD in math?" she added, grinning broadly.

Allie blinked. "Wait. You're dating someone who's a doctor, and a math nerd?"

Molly snorted, trying not to laugh. "Yeah, I am, and he is, very."

"About time," Allie told her.

"Mo–om!"

"Don't Mo–om me," Allie repeated. "Your last few boyfriends have been sadly lacking in the brains department."

"Yeah, well, it's not like brains are exactly a requirement in Hollywood. Pretty, yes. Smarts? Not so much."

Like Riley. The man was lovely to look at, but he was an ass and an idiot. Not that he had ever been a dating prospect, despite Ricki's machinations. But Fountain. Fountain was —perfect.

"So, tell me, this doctor of yours, is he cute?"

"Oh god, yes! Although he doesn't know it!"

Allie laughed. "Men always know when they're good looking, honey."

"Not Rhodes, trust me."

Allie titled her head slightly. "You call him Rhodes?"

Molly shrugged. "When I met him that's what he told me to call him, so, yeah, I do. Mostly." Except when they were kissing, or—

"Okayyyy, that's weird."

"Yeah, a little," Molly agreed.

"So, what does your handsome Dr. Rhodes do with his mismatched doctorates?"

Molly grinned, her mom was going to love this. "He works for the FBI!"

Allie blinked, her expression priceless, before she giggled. "Wait. You're dating one of the 'Men in Black'?" And images of starched white shirts, narrow ties and sunglasses danced through Molly's head.

"N—no!" she choked out, overcome with giggles herself. "Well, yes, except he doesn't dress like in the movies. He's more of a tweed jacket kind of guy. Like an absent-minded professor." She frowned for a minute, realizing something. "You know, I almost never see him in a suit. Not even when he's picked me up straight from work."

"Maybe, since he's a shrink, he doesn't always have to wear one?" Allie suggested.

"Yeah, maybe."

"So, where on earth did you meet him?" Allie asked. Such a typical 'mom' question, Molly thought fondly, and with a lot of giggles, Molly told her about their first meeting in the garden and the subsequent lunches that had followed. And the dinners that had come after that. And the weekend at his family's beach house.

Eight glorious weeks of stolen moments, stolen kisses, stolen nights together as her movie had filmed in and around D.C.

"So, when do I get to meet your not–Man in Black?" Allie asked.

Molly glanced at her watch. "How does half an hour sound?" she answered, a mischievous smile tugging at her lips.

"What!"

Molly laughed. "I haven't seen him in over a week, Mom! He got called out of state to work on something just as we were wrapping things up on the set, and I've missed him so much. He called to say he was back in town right as I was pulling into the driveway here, and since he has the next few days off, I invited him up for the weekend."

"Well, in that case, I'll go make myself scarce. I have some errands I can run in town, and Jenny wanted me to come over for tea, so I'll go do that. Give you two love birds some time alone together before I get back."

"Mom! You did not just say that! Love birds, really? Yuck! Although, 'yes, please' to you having tea with Aunt Jenny but stay for lunch first, okay? I really want you to meet him, and we might, um, not be here when you get back. We kinda talked about going away someplace," she added blushing hotly.

Allie raised an eyebrow. "You do know you don't have to 'go away' just because I'm here, right? It's not like I'm going to hear anything you two might get up to halfway across the house in the guest room."

"Mom! Stop!" Molly yelled, covering her ears, blushing even harder. "And that is so not happening."

"Well, it might, especially if you invite him to visit over the holidays."

"Mom, *stop!*"

"Fine." Allie said serenely. "So, what are you feeding Dr. Wonderful, seeing as how it's almost lunch time?" She asked, changing the subject.

With a relieved sigh Molly said, "I've got it covered. Just answer the door when he gets here. Oh, and Mom? Be nice, please?"

Which made Allie laugh. "I promise not to scare him away," she promised.

"Mrs. Whittier? I'm Fountain Rhodes," the young man said, introducing himself when she answered the door a short time later.

"It's nice to meet you, Fountain," Allie said pleasantly, stepping aside so he could come in. She had no intention of calling him Rhodes. That was just ridiculous.

Dressed in a dark gray tweed jacket, navy blue cords, a mauve shirt patterned with small flowers and a dark burgundy tie, she had to agree with Molly that Fountain Rhodes couldn't have looked less like one of the infamous "Men in Black" if he'd tried. The absent-minded-professor look, however, he had down pat. He was also every bit as good looking as Molly had said he was. He could have been a movie star with his rumpled curls and five o'clock shadow.

But it was his eyes that caught Allie's attention. They were heavily bruised from fatigue, and the man looked exhausted. She wondered what it was he did, exactly, for the FBI.

"Molly's back here," she said, inviting him to follow her down the long hallway to the huge sun-drenched kitchen where Molly was singing along to the radio as she stood at the center island chopping up celery.

It wasn't until she was halfway across the room that Allie realized Rhodes had paused in the doorway, simply drinking in the sight of Molly.

"Oh, I thought I heard the doorbell," Molly started to say, before she turned her head, caught sight of Rhodes and let the knife fall from her fingers. It clattered noisily on the chopping board as she started toward him.

He met her halfway, sweeping her up into his arms, and Allie had to hide her grin at the way they simply held each other as if they couldn't bear to be apart ever again. And the thought crossed her mind that she'd never seen her daughter so smitten before, ever, by anyone.

"Missed you," Rhodes whispered, brushing a hand over her hair.

"Missed you too," Molly whispered back softly, slipping her arms under his jacket, and to Allie, it seemed as if the weight of the world slid off Rhodes's shoulders at her touch. For a minute, they just stood there, arms wrapped tightly around each other, before he let her go again and took a step back, as if he suddenly remembered they weren't alone.

"God, Rhodes, you look exhausted. When was the last time you slept?" Molly exclaimed, taking a good look at him.

"I snuck a few hours in here and there and a few more on the plane back this morning."

"You shouldn't have driven up here."

"I'm fine, Moll," he said smiling. "I wouldn't have risked driving if I'd been too tired."

And as they laced their fingers together, Allie thought that smitten worked both ways, because this young man was more than smitten with her daughter—he was in love with her whether he knew it or not yet.

"So, you wanna help chop?" Molly asked drawing him over to the counter and picking up the knife again.

"Ummm, no." Rhodes answered, pulling out a counter stool and sitting down. "I like my fingers where they are just fine."

"Hmmm, burns breakfast and can't chop vegetables without causing serious harm to himself," Molly teased.

Does he now? Allie thought, wondering when he'd burned breakfast for Molly. At the beach, maybe?

"But I do know how to vacuum and dust," he shot back, a smile hovering on his lips.

"A veritable domestic god," she agreed.

"Fountain, can I pour you some wine?" Allie asked, moving over to the island and pouring herself and Molly each a glass.

"Um . . ." he hesitated for a moment before sighing. "No, thank you, Ms. Whittier. I better not. I'd probably just fall asleep if I had one right now. But I wouldn't say no to a glass of water."

Allie smiled, "Fountain, please, call me Allie."

"Yes, ma'am." And when she rolled her eyes, he blushed and said, "Yes, Allie."

Much later, Allie chased them out of the kitchen into the sunroom.

"Go," she shooed. And they went, fingers twining as they walked away.

A smile crossed her face. They made a handsome couple she thought, and she knew exactly what had attracted Molly to Fountain. He was a lot like her brother, Michael—another warm, caring man, who was also exceptionally brilliant, though perhaps not quite in the way that Fountain was. No, she suspected that when it came to brilliance, Dr. Fountain Rhodes might very well be in a league of his own.

When she peeked in on them later, Molly was sitting on the floor on a pile of giant pillows, back up against the couch, reading from a small red leather-bound book as she ran her fingers through Rhodes's hair. Rhodes, himself, was sprawled out, sound asleep beside her, his head in her lap, looking like he was all of sixteen.

Allie slipped silently away, a smile on her face. As far as she was concerned, Fountain Rhodes was a keeper.

FIVE
THE KISS

What was wrong with people? Didn't they watch horror movies? Didn't they know what was going to happen to them if they cut through a dark alley, alone, in the middle of the night with no one around to hear them scream?

It was almost funny, really, how shocked the guy had been when he stuck a knife into him. And why had he said, "No! Please?" after he'd already done it? Made no sense. He hadn't even struggled. He'd just sort of stiffened, then toppled over, without even a whimper. The guy had probably been as boring in life as he'd been in death. No great loss then.

Still, he could have at least struggled a bit. It had been kind of like skipping the foreplay and just jumping ahead to the sex. If he'd wanted that, he would have paid a hooker, then taken the money back after he'd killed her. But, yeah, no. Every Tom, Dick, and Harry wanna-be serial killer did that. Far more entertaining to be spontaneous.

He looked down at the knife he still held in his hand and frowned. What was he supposed to do with it now? It wasn't like he could just toss it in his backpack all wet and drippy. Huh. Well, that was irritating. He hadn't actually thought about that before he'd come out tonight, but he didn't want to just leave it. He liked *this knife. God, who knew killing people took so much planning?*

He closed his eyes for a moment reliving the feel of the kill. It was so much better than the shooting one. More personal? Hmmm, he'd have to try the gun again to be sure. But strangling as an MO was most definitely out. That had been—yeah, once was enough. He thought briefly about the time he'd hit the old woman over the head with a hammer, but, no, that hadn't done it for him either. She just— died. One minute there and the next, compost in her garden. Maybe because she'd been old? Maybe he should try it again with someone younger. And a baseball bat.

But the knife. Oh, the knife was just like making love, only better. No yippety, yappity, yap after. No, "when can I see you again?" shit. Just in, out, done. Forever. Yeah, he'd definitely be using a knife again, once he figured out what to do with it after. Speaking of which. He looked around and grinned. He was in the alley behind the Soul Garden Café, where he worked. How fortuitous was that? Considering the café supplied newspapers to its morning customers and there they were, stacks of them, all neatly tied together waiting to be recycled. He grabbed a bundle and wedged the knife deep into the center of the thing and gave it a shake. Perfect. And now to get his trophy. But the guy proved to be as worthless in death as he'd been in life, having only a run-of-the-mill door key on him. Ah well, killers couldn't be choosers, he told himself. Besides, he didn't have anything this boring in his collection yet, so now he did.

Flipping it back and forth across his fingers, he picked up the newspaper bundle with his other hand and took one last look around. Good thing the café had closed a while ago, or he might have run into the night manager. Now that would have been awkward. Especially with a dead guy at his feet.

Giving the key one last flip before pushing it into the front pocket of his jeans, he sauntered out of the alley, catching the barest whiff of onions cooking on the crisp night air. Soooo good, that smell. His stomach rumbled in agreement. Tacos, it told him. It wanted tacos, and there was a taco truck just a few blocks over that stayed open 24/7. Perfect. He'd get a snack and then go home. Maybe he'd get a horchata too—he'd always liked those.

"Please tell me that that antique hunk of junk out front does not belong to our dear Dr. Rhodes," Michael Whittier asked his mother with a quick glance around the brightly lit kitchen to be sure they were alone. A lopsided smile graced his handsome face as he gave her a quick hug. Six feet tall, he shared his sister's dark brown hair and ocean blue eyes, a legacy from their father. His quick wit and genius he'd gotten from his mother, but his love for all things mathematic was his alone.

Something delicious was cooking in the oven, and the aroma of hot mulled cider drew him over to the stove top to pour a cup. God, he loved the holidays. The drinks, the food, the three weeks off from school with nothing to do but whatever he wanted to.

Allie Whittier smiled at her oldest child fondly. "Yes," she said simply, "it does."

"Wow, he's braver than I thought!" Michael said, snagging a stool at the counter and sitting down so they could keep talking while she continued kneading the dough that he suspected was going to become an apple pie crust, judging by the other ingredients on the counter.

"Be nice," Allie chided. "He's not just a Federal Agent, you know. He also has a doctorate in mathematics, like someone else I know," she added looking at him pointedly.

Michael stared at his mother, shocked. He'd known the man was a Federal Agent and a shrink, but he hadn't known Rhodes had a PhD in mathematics too. Why hadn't he known that? he thought, followed rapidly by—just great. The guy was probably also an insufferably smug jackass, seeing as how he was all three. But what he said was, "So . . . *what?* That means he knows where the gas tank is?"

"Michael! Be nice!" Allie repeated, but she was laughing when she said it.

He cocked his head and looked at her. Really looked at her. Oh my god, he thought. "You *like* him!"

Allie nodded. "Yes. I do," she said simply.

Taking a gulp of his cider, Michael considered his mother's answer as he swirled the sweet hot drink around his mouth, savoring the flavors while a million thoughts scrambled through his brain. Never, not once, had his mom liked someone Molly had dated. *Ever*. Huh. So, what was it about this guy that she liked? What made him so special? Other than the fact he was smart and probably good looking and—at a complete loss, he asked her.

Allie smiled. "He just . . . is."

"Wow, Mom, that was helpful!"

"Why don't you go find out for yourself? They're down in The Kingdom," she told him.

The Kingdom. Michael grinned despite himself. Years ago, Molly had proclaimed the sunroom her own 'private kingdom' and the name had stuck, even after all these years.

"To the Kingdom it is then," he said, wondering why on earth he felt so unnerved about meeting one of Molly's boyfriends. They'd never rattled him before. Not a single muscle-bound, Neanderthal one of them.

Yeah, but Mom had never *liked* one of them before, he whined mentally. *Get a grip!* He admonished himself. What the heck was *wrong* with hm? Was he scared the guy was going to beat him up or something? Molly's nerdy, genius, older brother.

Ah geez, he hadn't felt this insecure since high school.

I'm older than he is, he thought childishly. Yeah, by a whole year, and—he'd been about to say smarter too. But he wasn't, was he? Just as smart, maybe, and that was something new. Molly had never dated someone as smart as he was before.

He paused in the dark hallway and grinned. *Wow, Whittier,*

he told himself, *way to be grownup!* Then he stepped into the doorway of Molly's Kingdom and stopped dead.

It wasn't just that Molly and Rhodes were kissing. It was the *way* they were kissing, with so much passion and tenderness that Michael's breath caught in his throat, and Molly heard him. In one fluid movement, she pushed away from her startled lover, snatched up a cushion and threw it at her brother.

"Oh, you *brat!*" she screamed. "How long have you been standing there?"

"Long enough to learn a few things about kissing I didn't know before!" he got out wickedly, barely dodging the second and third cushions that sailed past him.

"Oh! Get *OUT!*" she yelled, throwing another cushion at him.

"It's my home too, sweetie," he reminded her, throwing a quick wink at a startled Dr. Rhodes before beating a hasty retreat back up the hallway, before his sister threw something hard and hurtful at him.

"Well?" Allie asked, as he walked back into the kitchen again.

"Well, what?"

"Michael!"

"We, uh, didn't exactly get a chance to meet," he admitted, grinning.

"Ah," his mom said, smiling despite herself, "I take it they were busy?"

"You could put it that way," he agreed. What he didn't say

was that Fountain Rhodes wasn't at all who he'd been expecting.

Nor was the way he'd been kissing his little sister.

Damn.

———

"Look at you, bearing gifts!" May LaGrange exclaimed, eyes fixed on the mocha latte Detective Tolliver had brought her. "Just put it on the desk. I'll be there in a minute," she added, stripping off the latex gloves and the mask she'd been wearing. A moment later, after having taken a large sip she said, "But I'm sorry, cher, I don't have anything else to add to what we already know about Mr. Tansig. He was stabbed with what looks like an ordinary kitchen knife, which we presume the killer then took away with him."

"Ah."

Crap, how was it the woman always stole his words away from him? He cast around for something intelligent to say but came up with nothing. Story of his life, so instead he just blurted, "Your hair looks nice." Which it did. But . . . *Christ.*

She smiled and patted the long, thick braid she'd curled round her head and said, "Really? Thank you. I'm thinking about getting dreads."

He frowned, trying to picture that, and she laughed. "No?" she asked.

"No. I mean, yes! I think they'd look good on you." As long as she didn't do anything weird like dye the ends red or purple.

She waited a heartbeat longer, laughter in her eyes, as if daring him to invite her out. But he still hadn't worked up the courage for that yet.

"Well, if that's all, I need to get back to work," she told him, and getting up on her toes, she kissed his cheek, then gave him a push toward the exit.

Michael noticed two things almost simultaneously about Molly's Dr. Rhodes when she dragged him into the kitchen a short time later. The first was that he was clearly embarrassed that Michael had caught them kissing, and the second was that he was clueless as to how to handle the situation. Which was interesting. If he hadn't known better, Michael would have said that Rhodes was acting, well, like *he* would have, but that wasn't possible was it? Molly's boyfriends had always been big, in-your-face kind of guys. Except—except Dr. Rhodes clearly wasn't like any of them.

In fact, Rhodes was so unlike anyone that Molly had ever dated before that it begged the question: had Molly finally traded in her muscle-bound boyfriends for someone, well, more nerdy, like he was? Because Molly's Dr. Rhodes looked *exactly* like a nerd. In fact, he looked like a *poster boy* for nerd. From his tweed jacket to his corduroy pants, the sweater vest, the flower-patterned shirt with the top button undone, and the slightly skewed tie as if he'd tugged it loose because it was strangling him. The messy curls and five o'clock shadow just added to the picture. He was the epitome of what a nerd should look like, if nerds were movie-star handsome, which the guy was, in spades.

"Dr. Rhodes, I presume?" Michael said, before the silence got awkward.

Rhodes cleared his throat. "Dr. Whittier?" he asked back, and then they both snickered at how ridiculous that sounded. Like they were a pair of puffed up buffoons. Or teenaged boys. Yup, the guy was definitely a nerd.

"Most people call me Whitt," Michael said, grinning widely.

"Most people call me Rhodes," Rhodes answered.

"Yeah, even your girlfriend," Whitt shot back. Which was when Allie stepped in.

"Whitt!" she admonished sharply, "behave!"

"I am!" he protested. "I'm exhibiting proper male, 'you're dating my sister and I need to know if you're worthy,' behavior."

"You going to pee on him next to mark your territory too?" Molly snickered.

"Actually, he'd pee on you," Rhodes said, as if the conversation were serious.

For a minute the kitchen went completely silent before Molly squealed, "Ew, that's gross!" and Michael and Rhodes burst out laughing like middle schoolers. *Oh yeah, I think I like this guy,* Michael thought, as they high fived, grinning at each other like idiots.

"So, did I pass the test?" Rhodes asked, accepting a glass of mulled cider from Molly.

"Of course you did," Molly said. "You're both morons."

"I believe the word you were looking for was geniuses?" Michael corrected.

Molly rolled her eyes, "If it makes you sleep better at night."

"Half an hour to dinner," Allie interrupted, smiling.

"In that case," Michael gestured to the cluster of couches and chairs at the end of the long, homey kitchen, "let's adjourn to the den."

"Why? So you can compare video games next?" Molly teased as she and Rhodes sat on the couch, while Michael and Allie took the squishy overstuffed armchairs.

"I don't play video games," the two men said together.

"Oh god, a match made in heaven. And you lie. Both of you," Molly added.

"*Mario Kart* doesn't count," they said again in unison.

"You know where this is going, now, don't you?" Allie asked Molly, smiling.

"Nowhere," Molly said firmly, taking Rhodes hand in hers. "We're going to sit here and pretend we're adults, not go haring off like teenagers to play video games."

"Easy for you to do," Michael grumbled under his breath. "You're an actress."

"Fountain, dear, why don't you take off your jacket and get

comfortable?" Allie said, cutting him off midgrumble, "And I'm so glad you can stay until Christmas."

"Thank you for inviting me," Rhodes answered, pulling off his tie, then stuffing it into a pocket as he stood up to take his jacket off.

Wow, Michael thought, he had not been expecting the gun under the man's arm. It kind of shattered the whole nerdy-vibe thing they'd had going on, reminding him exactly what it was the man did for a living.

"So, Rhodes, are you planning on shooting dinner?" he asked as nonchalantly as he could.

Obviously confused, Rhodes frowned for a minute before he got it. Then confused turned to flustered. "No! Oh god, I'm so sorry. I just—it's just, *shit*," he muttered, much to Michael's amusement. "I'll just go, um, get rid of it."

"Fountain, you're a Federal Agent. You wear a gun. It's fine." Allie told him, shooting Michael a glare first.

"Yes, I am—I do—but not in the house. I always take it off as soon as I get home. I just—got distracted. I'm so sorry."

Michael couldn't quite keep the sly grin from tugging at his lips as he said, "So, that's what all the hip kids are calling it, now, are they? Getting *distracted?*"

"God, it's like you're ten years old sometimes!" Molly snapped.

"He started it," Michael sing-songed back.

"The two of you are like a match made in heaven," Molly muttered, a few minutes later, as Fountain slipped his gun and harness into his duffle bag. They were in the small guest room just off the sunroom. "You're such dorks."

"And that's—a good thing?" Rhodes asked uncertainly, as he turned toward her.

"A very good thing," she reassured him.

"Well, in that case, I will embrace my inner dorkiness," he told her, pulling her into his arms and sending shivers down her spine as he ghosted his lips against hers.

Oh god, yes, if this is your version of dorkiness, embrace it, she thought, *please?* And as if he'd read her mind he nibbled and licked at her bottom lip. She couldn't keep back her whimper, didn't even try to and suddenly his lips were pressed hard against hers, his tongue insistent, demanding entrance. She let him in, heart pounding, loving the possessive way his tongue plundered her mouth, driving her senseless.

Then he slid a hand beneath her sweater, and as his fingers stroked across her back, she forgot how to think completely. His fingertips dancing across her spine, her ribs, the touch familiar now, their tips rough, catching on her skin, igniting her, leaving a trail of fire wherever they skimmed.

"Oh god," she whimpered when he pulled his mouth away from hers. She wasn't done kissing him yet. Didn't think she'd ever be done. She was addicted to the taste of him, to the smell of him, something light and citrusy that brushed across her senses as he cupped the side of her face and stroked her cheek with his thumb before he danced it lightly across her bottom lip. She flicked her tongue out, licking it, and felt him catch his breath. Just one simple touch, and he was as undone as she was.

For a brief moment he rested his forehead against hers, and she could feel him trembling. He pulled her closer yet, pressing his body to hers, then his mouth was dipping back down, butterfly soft kisses dancing against her lips. She moaned, and the sound seemed to ignite him, his mouth crushing against hers. Tongues warred and licked, teeth bit and lips grew swollen and sore before they parted panting for breath. Then he claimed her lips all over again, his mouth hot, needy, impassioned.

But she wanted more, needed more, needed—yes, that—as he tugged on her shirt, dragging it free of her skirt, all thoughts of dinner forgotten. Dear god, she thought, right before she stopped thinking at all as his hands slipped underneath her camisole and cupped her breasts, squeezing, caressing, his thumbs brushing her nipples, bringing them to hardened, aching, peaks.

"Molly," he moaned, biting down on her lip. She would have screamed in desire if he hadn't covered her mouth just then with his own, his tongue seeking, probing. Her senses shattered, and when they finally parted, his beautiful eyes were heavy lidded, hot with lust and a need of his own.

"Oh god, Rhodes," she breathed, fisting her hands in his hair and pulling his mouth down to hers again. She could kiss him forever.

When they broke apart this time, Rhodes buried his face in her neck, the stubble on his cheek rough against her skin. She loved the way it felt. His head dipped as he nibbled and tasted and licked his way down to the hollow of her throat and gently sucked on the tender skin there. Then his lips were back on hers again, taking tiny, gentle sips as she trailed feather light fingers down his chest, feeling his muscles tightening with the friction of his shirt as she trailed them down lower still, covering his moans with ones of her own.

"*Molly*," it was barely a plea. He wanted her, wanted her as much as she wanted him.

And then his phone rang. The opening bars of *Duty Calls,* by Broken Wings swirling around them. The song he'd assigned to Page. Her hand stilled on the flat planes of his belly. His lips slid from hers. For a bare moment, he rested their foreheads together. No . . . not *now,* she thought. They'd promised him four whole days off. The noise stopped.

She hated to ask, but she had to. "Rhodes?" He shook his head, tracing circles on her back with shaking hands, then it rang again. Moaning in frustration, he dug it out of his pocket, setting it down on the bedside table unanswered, before pulling her against him again.

"I'm sorry," he whispered against her lips as he feathered another soft kiss against them. When it rang again, he groped blindly for it, his voice hoarse, husky as he answered it, hitting speaker phone so he could keep Molly close to him.

"Why didn't you answer the first time I called?" Page's voice was sharp, annoyed, loud over the speaker.

For a moment, Fountain didn't respond. "I didn't have my phone on me. I'm on vacation," he reminded the man, gently. She would have yelled at Page, but that wasn't Rhodes's way.

A pause. "I'm sorry."

Rhodes blinked, the apology unexpected.

Then Pages's voice, brisk, authoritative, weary, Molly thought. "We have a missing child. I need you to do the follow-up interviews. Too many family members who don't know anything. No tire tracks in the snow out front and too many sled tracks out the back to follow where they lead."

Molly's eyes widened, and she felt Rhodes fingers gently take hers and squeeze, before he stepped away from her and let them go.

"Your flight leaves in twenty-five minutes," Page added.

"Page—I'm not in Alexandria. I'm in Front Royal." Rhodes said hurriedly, before the man hung up on him.

"You're *where?*"

Rhodes didn't bother repeating himself, the question had been rhetorical. They could hear Page talking rapidly to someone else, before he came back on the line and said, "I need an address."

"Um . . ." Rhodes gave it to him, stuttering slightly. Clearly at a loss as to why until Page said, "Is there somewhere to put down a chopper there?"

A—*what?* Molly thought.

Rhodes glanced over his shoulder. Through the open bedroom doorway, across the adjacent sunroom, Molly knew he could see the garden. "Yeah, there's probably an acre out back. The trees won't be a problem and there aren't any power lines," he added, while Molly stared at him, eyes wide as she realized what was going on.

"ETA?" Page barked at someone else. Then to Rhodes he said, "The chopper's scrambling out of Winchester, it'll be on its way in a couple of minutes. I'll see they hold your flight at Dulles. And Rhodes . . . I'm sorry," he added tiredly.

A sentiment Rhodes echoed seconds later as he tossed his phone onto the bed. Reaching out, he pulled her back toward him, gently stroking her cheek with the back of his fingers, before lowering his head and claiming her mouth again. "I really am sorry," he whispered.

"No," she shook her head, tears in her eyes. A missing child. At Christmas. "No sorries," she told him. God, was there anything more horrible?

He nodded, then turning to his bag, pulled out his gun and shoulder harness and slipped them on again. When he pulled her back into his arms moments later and pressed their lips together, she deepened the kiss, giving him what he wanted. What he needed. Reassurance, love, understanding, until they were both wrung out and breathless.

"You think your mom's going to get mad when a helicopter lands in her garden?" he asked.

Wha . . . what? Molly blinked, still dizzy from his kisses. "I . . . I think she'll get over it," she breathed finally.

Oh mercy, he was *leaving,* and he'd only just gotten here. "Rhodes!"

"I'm sorry," he whispered again.

She bowed her head against his chest, fighting tears as he wrapped his arms around her, then she pulled away slowly and looked up at him. God, he was a mess. Hair every which way, lips bruised and swollen.

"You look like you've been mangled," she told him.

He laughed, a teasing smile on his face. "I feel like it, too," he told her. Then the smile faded slowly as he touched her lips with his fingertips, before he reached into his pocket and pulled out his keys.

"You might need to move my car before I can send someone to get it."

She took them from him reluctantly, twining her fingers in his. "Or you could just leave it."

"I could. But I don't know how long I'll be gone."

She blinked back selfish tears. "I'm not going anywhere until after Christmas. It'll be safe here. I promise."

He brushed his lips across her forehead before nodding. "Okay, then," he said softly, before pulling her against him again. "Apologize to your mom for me?" he whispered. "Dinner smelled delicious."

"I'll freeze some for you," she said, trying to lighten the

moment, and got the little chuckle she was hoping for. Then his lips were on hers again and everything else was forgotten.

The whumping sound of beating rotors cut through the air not long after, and with a heavy heart, Rhodes stepped away from Molly to watch it. The chopper landing in a wash of leaves and flower petals.

Mrs. Whittier's going to kill me, he thought as he watched the destruction of her flower beds, bushes whipping every which way in the wash from the rotors. Beside him, Molly slid her hand into his, desperately holding on. For a second, their eyes met before he lowered his head for one last mind searing kiss. Then, snatching up his jacket and bag, he quickly crossed into the sunroom, then let himself out into the yard and ran across it, ducking his head low to run under the whirring blades. When he looked back, Molly was standing in the open doorway, watching him go.

He tore his gaze away, climbing aboard, slamming the door, strapping himself in before jamming the headset on. When the pilot swung the chopper around as they lifted up, he got a last glimpse of Molly looking up at him, and his heart did something complicated inside his chest.

"Hot chick," the pilot said as they headed east, and she disappeared somewhere behind them.

You have no idea, Rhodes thought. You have no idea at all.

SIX

CHOICES

EARLY JANUARY

The problem with winter was it rained. And who wanted to kill someone in the rain? It dripped down the back of your neck if the coat you were wearing didn't have a hood, so you had to wear a hat. And he hated hats. But, if you wore a coat with a hood you lost your peripheral vision, which wasn't a good idea if you were planning on killing someone. Umbrellas were also out because—how the hell would you even do that he wondered?

He pictured himself with an umbrella, the long metal tip sharpened to a fine point, sliding it into someone's unsuspecting body like a sword, while the rain poured down on him and—it got stuck, or it suddenly opened, or—yeah, no, that so wasn't happening, and it wasn't like he could juggle an umbrella and a knife at the same time.

Using a gun for a random kill was out too. Not just because the rain would make the grip all slippery, but because a gun was— personal. Something you used when you knew the person you were about to kill, like dear Professor Stone. Not that he'd actually killed her, yet. He was still thinking about it. Miserable bitch.

Which left a knife, and he did love the intimacy of a knife, but today he had something else entirely different in his pocket, something he'd decided on specifically for today's adventure. Something that was going to make the medical examiner gasp when they found it. Now, if it would only stop raining long enough that he could actually kill somebody with it . . .

He drummed his fingers on the table, in counterpoint to the rain beating against the coffee shop window, knowing how annoying he was being. Which was kinda the point.

He was sitting next to a group of knitters, waiting for one of them to tell him to stop. But they didn't, they just threw him angry glances, then looked away quickly to resume their cackling and clicking and "in a minute"s and, "I'm counting"s and—god, they reminded him of his mother. In a minute. In a minute. In a minute. I'm counting. I'm counting. One, Two, Three, knit two together, Five. One, Two, Three, knit two together, Five. The words and numbers keeping time with the rain, until he wanted to slaughter the whole pack of them. But none of them took the bait.

Finally, he got bored of waiting and got up and stretched. Little did they know today had been their lucky day. If one of them had complained, he would have killed them. Well, not here in the coffee shop but outside in the parking lot. Rain or no rain. A quick stab in the ribs as they got into their car with the lovely metal knitting needle he had in his pocket. He could almost feel it. A quick jab and twist as he guided it completely in and up through the heart. He snickered to himself, wishing he could be there to see the ME's face when they discovered it.

Of course, first he had to kill someone with it, but he had all day to find his perfect victim. It wasn't like there weren't about a million coffee shops all with the requisite knit groups in them. And what was with that? His mom had always knitted alone, at home. Maybe she would have lived longer if she'd had somewhere else to be besides home all day, moaning and whining about having to cook and clean. Then again, maybe not.

She sure as hell wouldn't have made the spicy chicken concoction that was currently bubbling away in the Crock-Pot for dinner, either. All her meals had been so bland they'd made him want to scream. Nope, he and Dad were so much better off without her. Best decision they'd ever made. Getting rid of her.

Speaking of decisions, he thought he'd pick up some beer on the way home. Something ice cold and dark would go great with the chicken, and Dad did love beer.

As he settled in at the next coffee shop, the rain began to taper off. Perfect. Yes, the day was definitely starting to look up, just like the pencil thin knitter with the bright red lips at the table beside him. She was not amused by his tap, tap, tapping. He gave her a wide, lazy grin and waited. It took her twenty minutes before she'd had enough. Shoving her knitting away, she said something sharp to her friends, cast him one last annoyed look and got up. Yes, today was really turning into a most lovely day, he thought, as he followed her out to the parking lot.

"What do you mean you're not going with Martin?" Ricki raged, her short red curls bouncing against her neck as she shook her head in disbelief. "You *have* to go with him! It's the Golden Globes, Molly!"

"I already told you, no!" Molly snarled back. "We've been over all this before! I am *not* going *anywhere* with that smug, vain, conceited, jerk breath of an actor!"

"Martin Riley is one of the hottest—"

"No."

"Best looking—"

"No."

"Actors around, and he—"

"*NO!*"

The two women glared at each other.

"I am *not* going with Martin Riley. I'm going with Michael! End of discussion."

"Fine!" Ricki hissed through clenched teeth. "But you are *not* going to the Oscars with your brother, do you hear me, Molly?"

"Fine!" she shot back. "But I'm not going with Riley, either!"

"What is it you don't understand about this?" Ricki snapped, hands gripping the curls at the top of her head. "You need to be seen with Riley! You need your face splashed across the tabloids with your costar. You need hints of a love affair to keep you in the spotlight. Being perfection on the big screen isn't enough.

People want something to gossip about, real or imagined. They want sex. Scandal. *Something.*"

"Fine! I'll give them something," Molly shouted. "But. Not. With. Riley!"

Detective Tolliver stared at the murder weapon May had removed from the victim. A knitting needle. An old fashioned, knitting needle like his mother had used. His second ex-wife had preferred wooden ones, and they weren't the straight kind like the killer had used but were circular, joined together by a thin nylon cord. But this one, this one was long and thin and straight and purple, and who killed someone with a knitting needle?

"You're kidding me," he said, looking at her in disbelief.

"I kid you not," she answered him. "Hands down the weirdest murder weapon I've ever seen."

"So, what, I'm looking for a pissed off knitter?"

May considered the question with the same seriousness she applied to everything. "No. I doubt it," she said finally. "Most knitters get mad at their knitting, not at each other. Not enough to kill them at least. And there'd be the whole 'messing up a pair of perfectly good knitting needles' thing. It's not like you can go out and buy just one."

Tolliver gave her a look.

She raised her eyebrows. "What? I knit. It's not an uncommon past time."

He huffed out a breath. He had not known that. Then again, there were a million things he didn't know about her. Yet. "So, that's all you've got for me?"

LaGrange took a sip of the mocha latte he'd had brought her, sighed happily, then said, "No. I can tell you the knitting needle was brought to the scene, since hers are in the sweater she was knitting, and are a different size, anyway. And that the killer wore gloves since there isn't so much as a smudge on the murder weapon."

Tolliver rubbed his eyes, shook his head and said, "So you're thinking someone planned on killing her?"

She cocked her head and thought about it as she took another sip of her coffee. "Not necessarily," she said finally. Then flashing him a grin, she added, "Could be it's just some looney with a flair for the dramatic."

He shot her an annoyed look, and she blew him a kiss, which made him feel all warm inside. He still had a grin on his face when he stepped out into the rain which had started up again while they'd been talking.

"Is this a good time? Because I'm having a really rotten morning," Molly asked, sounding more than a little annoyed by whatever had happened to her.

Pushing slightly away from his desk, Fountain glanced at the clock on his laptop, did the math, and saw it wasn't even eight o'clock yet out in Hawaii where Molly was.

"Yeah, actually it is," he told her, tossing the remains of his late lunch into the trash can beside him. She couldn't have timed her call any better. "So, what's happened?"

"It's Ricki. She's driving me crazy again," Molly exclaimed, launching right into a replay of her conversation with Ricki, and Fountain couldn't help grinning, just a little, at her outrage as he leaned back in his chair and settled his cell phone more comfortably against his ear.

In his mind's eye, he could see Molly clearly, tugging on her hair, eyes flashing fire as she paced back and forth. Or at least he assumed she was pacing, seeing as how her voice got fainter than louder again as she talked to him. Which meant her hands were probably waving about wildly, since he was obviously on speaker. "She was trying to match me up with Martin again, for The Globes!" she finished furiously.

"What do you want me to do, Moll, shoot him for you?" Rhodes asked, laughing. He wasn't entirely sure what the big deal was. She didn't have to like the man to go to an award show with him.

"That would work," she grumbled. "'Cause now she's going to try to make me go to the Oscars with him, I just know it. Why will she not listen to the fact that I have no intention of ever being seen alone with him? She's still trying to make it seem like we're a 'thing.' Maybe you should go with me, instead, so she'll finally get it through her head that that's never happening!"

What? Rhodes stared at his phone. He had not heard her right.

"Oh god," she said softly, "Wait."

And Fountain thought, *NO,* guessing where this was heading.

"How could I have been so stupid? Rhodes, that's it! And it's the perfect time and place, not to mention it would put an end to this Martin Riley nonsense!"

The perfect time and place . . . dear god, she was serious!

They'd talked about his "coming out," as Molly had put it, before. Talked about manipulating the time and the place and the press to make it easier on him when they told the world they were dating. But they had *not* talked about the *Academy Awards.* He closed his eyes. The Academy Awards, with half the world watching. *This* was the perfect place?

"Rhodes, it really is perfect. Think about it." Molly's voice was earnest, excited. "There's so much happening at the Oscars. It wouldn't just be about you and me. We'd just be a small part of it."

"Molly—"

"And it's not like I've been nominated for anything this year," she plowed on.

He swallowed hard, because no, this year she hadn't been, but her unspoken, "next year" hovered between them, because next year everyone expected her to get a Best Actress nomination for the movie she'd worked on all summer with Martin Riley. The movie that was currently number one at the box office.

Nominated or not, he couldn't. "Molly, I don't—"

"You haven't even thought it through!" she interrupted. "Just take a minute. Please?"

Okay. She had a point. He hadn't. He'd just reacted blindly to the notion.

He took a deep breath and let it out again, slowly. And after a minute, he realized she was right. In all the madness that was the awards, the focus wouldn't be on them, not with all the hoopla that surrounded it. The reporters would be fixated on what clothes the celebrities were wearing, their hair, their jewels, whether or not they were drunk, or stoned or . . . He opened his eyes slowly, not sure when he'd closed them. This was crazy, he told himself. *He* was crazy to even be considering it.

"I need to talk to Page," he heard himself say. What if he was knee deep in the middle of a case? Could he just leave it and fly to Hollywood for the evening? Would the Bureau allow that? Would the Bureau allow any of it?

A voice interrupted his thinking, and it wasn't Molly's. "Here are the files you asked for," it said, as the owner of the voice dropped a folder on his desk.

He gave a thank-you nod as the man hurried off, then apologetically said, "Molly, I—"

"Have to go," Molly finished for him. "But you'll think about it, right? And you'll talk to Page?" she added softly. "Rhodes?" she prompted when he didn't answer right away.

"Yes," he promised, and for a brief instant he wondered if he could get away with "Dad, can I take Molly to the Academy Awards ceremony?" as his opening statement, before he dismissed it for several reasons. The first being Page really didn't like it when they called him Dad to his face.

It took Rhodes a while to realize he'd been staring at the same sheet of paper for the last ten minutes while Molly's words chased themselves around in his head. Finally, with a deep-seated sigh, he pushed the offending report away.

"Everything all right?" His new teammate, Nico Romano, asked. He was sitting on the edge of Gia Talafiero's desk, coffee mug in one hand, file in the other, as if he were working instead of flirting. While Gia pretended she wasn't listening as she peered at the columns of numbers on her computer screen. The three of them had only just started working together in some kind of reorganization no one seemed to know anything about, but that had come down from on high.

In his mind, Fountain had dubbed the pair the "Italian Mafia." Romano looked like he could have been an old-fashioned mob boss with his slicked back dark hair and steely, almost-black eyes, Roman nose and perpetually stubbled square jaw. He was a sharp dresser too. His black suits perfectly tailored to show off his wide shoulders and slim waist.

Talafiero, on the other hand, was an Italian beauty with her rich olive skin, a perfect oval face and full rose-colored lips.

Thick eyelashes framed a pair of sharp, dark eyes. She also favored sharply tailored suits, but in her case, they showed off her tiny waist and legs that went on forever—not that he'd looked. But it was kind of hard not to.

Molly had laughed when he'd told her. "Looking's good for the soul," she'd told him, "just as long as that's all you do."

Still, he had wondered why they'd been transferred together out of the L.A. office. Even if they had been partners there, that was unusual enough in itself. The "we're rearranging teams" BS they'd been fed hadn't fooled anyone. Something was going on. Something that was being kept under wraps. Just like his relationship with Molly . . .

"Trouble in paradise?" Romano added, mouth twitching slightly as he tried to hide a grin. They'd barely gotten past shaking hands and exchanging names, before the fact that Rhodes was dating Molly Whittier had slipped out.

Two Weeks Earlier

Rhodes stood with his nose mere inches from the white board in front of him. Pictures of crime scenes and victims were pinned to it. He leaned in closer, myopic eyes focusing on the tiny detail in the photograph before him. Then spinning around suddenly, he dug through the stacks of printouts that were strewn across the large table behind him, found what he was looking for, stared at it, then turned back to the white board again.

Behind him, sitting at various places around the table, were his new teammates, Romano and Talafiero. They were plowing through the stacks of paper that pertained to the case they were working on. As was Page. All hands on deck for this one. Three couples, picked seemingly at random, had been slaughtered in their houses. The Arlington police had called them in to assist, but so far they'd come up with nothing that tied any of the dead together.

Rubbing his eyes, he sat back down and rummaged through the papers in front of where he'd been sitting. There was something hovering just on the edge of his consciousness, something he couldn't quite grab on to yet.

When his phone rang, he answered it the same way he always did. "Fountain Rhodes," he said briskly, like he wasn't exhausted from the hours they'd already spent pouring over the information they'd accumulated.

He hadn't been expecting Molly's familiar husky voice whispering, "Hello, sexy," and he couldn't help the laugh that slipped out, or the blush that crossed his cheeks.

Intensely aware of his new team members staring at him avidly, he walked out of the conference room as nonchalantly as possible before answering.

"Hey."

"Hey, yourself," she laughed, and he couldn't help smiling. "So, what are you doing?"

"Working," he admitted, sighing heavily as he leaned against a nearby wall.

"Poor Rhodes," she commiserated, although he caught the tiniest hint of laughter in her words.

"Yup, poor me, and it's *Sunday!*"

"Which makes it different from Monday, how?"

"Two letters," he countered, "S and U."

"Case has you stumped, huh?" she said gently.

He rubbed his temples, trying to ease the pounding headache that still lingered despite the ibuprofen he'd taken.

"Yes and no. There's something right there, but it's just out of reach."

"You need to eat."

He blinked, his mind having started to drift along a different path entirely.

"It's, uh," he glanced at his watch, "only five-thirty."

"Un huh," she agreed. "So, what's for dinner?"

Rhodes shrugged even though she couldn't see him. "I don't know, pizza, maybe?"

"Yuck. You need brain food. So, how many of you are there?"

He'd blinked. *Brain food?* "Um, four if you include Page."

"Well, you can't exclude your Assistant Special Agent in Charge," she teased. "So how bad is the headache?" Like she could hear it in his voice, which she probably could.

"On a scale of one to ten? About a seven," he admitted.

"Ow," she said sympathetically.

But just talking to Molly made it hurt less somehow.

"So, uh, how's Tahiti?" he asked, hoping he had the right location for her whereabouts. She'd started shooting her new movie right after Christmas, without even a break for New Year's Eve, which they'd spent on the phone together. And god, he missed her.

"Remote," she answered dryly, "and hot and sweaty."

"Sounds lovely."

"Yeah, if you like sand in your teeth. It's been really windy."

"I think I'll pass." There'd been no sand in their teeth when they'd gone to the beach the one time together. The hot and sweaty bit, though, they'd managed nicely. Damn. He tore his mind away from those memories.

"Miss you," she said quietly, her mind obviously on their trip too. "When's your next vacation? Maybe we could come back here, together. It would be lovely with *you*."

He caught her slight inflection and couldn't help the little grin that slid across his lips. He supposed paradise wasn't paradise when Martin Riley was in the picture. Literally, since he was her costar again.

God, he'd love to spend a week in Tahiti with Molly. Or two. Hell, he'd be happy to spend a week with her at his home in Alexandria, tucked up in his room or garden or—shit. "What's a vacation?" he asked instead. He honestly couldn't remember the last time he'd had a real one.

"Rhodes, they have to cut you loose sometime!"

He chuckled, then caught sight of Page walking back into the conference room and sighed. He hadn't even seen him leave.

"Time to go?" she asked, catching his sigh.

"Time to go," he agreed, wishing it were otherwise.

"Later," she said simply and hung up her phone. She'd learned early on that there would be no long goodbyes when he was on a case.

"So?" Romano asked, the second he walked back into the room.

"So, I think there's something we're missing about the houses," he answered, hiding a grin, knowing Romano was referring to his phone call and not the case.

"Rhodes—"

He cut Romano off, his mind already sliding from Molly to that niggling feeling. "There's something—" He grabbed the photographs of the house fronts and began pinning them to the wall. Before he was done, Molly was long forgotten.

"Uh, Agent Rhodes?" a young agent poked his head in through the doorway sometime later.

"Yes?"

"Your dinner's here."

His *what?* He looked around as the man slipped into the room with a large cooler in his hands. Romano quickly cleared a place in front of himself for it.

"Uh, what do I owe you?" Rhodes asked, patting his pockets in an effort to locate his wallet. He'd had no idea anyone had ordered dinner already or stuck him with the bill for it.

"No charge, sir," the young man answered sidling toward the doorway. "A Miss Whittier already paid for it."

What? He looked at the cooler confused. Molly had sent him dinner—from *Tahiti?*

"Miss Whittier, huh?" Romano had teased. "Well, let's see what's in here—ah, sushi," and Rhodes laughed.

"Brain food!" he explained quickly. "Molly said we needed brain food to figure out what we're missing about this case."

"*Molly*, huh?" Romano said, grin deepening. "Molly Whittier . . ." And then his smile faltered. "Oh no, no way. We're not talking *the* Molly Whittier, are we Rhodes? Like as in the movie star?"

"Yes," Page answered dryly for Rhodes, who was blushing deeply. "*The* Molly Whittier."

Which is when they'd found out who he was dating.

The Present

Rhodes sighed, pulling his thoughts away from Molly. Thinking about her only made him miss her even more desperately. They hadn't seen each other in weeks, and while the movie shoot had moved from Tahiti to Hawaii, which was a hell of a lot closer, with neither one of them able to shake loose, she might as well have been on the moon.

"Rhodes?" Romano prodded.

"No, everything's fine," he said, rubbing his eyes. "I just . . . I need to talk to Page."

Romano leaned out into the aisle between Gia's desk and Fountain's so he could see around them to Page's office. "So, go talk to him. He's alone right now."

A tentative knock on his open door followed by "Um, Page? Can I ask you something?" brought Page's attention to the man hovering in his doorway.

"Of course," he answered immediately, setting aside the file he'd been reading. It had only taken one look at Rhodes's troubled face to get his full attention. "Have a seat."

"Umm . . . it's about Molly." Rhodes said, without preamble.

Page raised an eyebrow. Well, that was unexpected.

"She's asked me to go to the Academy Awards with her, and . . . I don't know what to tell her."

Page sat perfectly still, staring at Rhodes as his bomb shell sunk in. She'd asked him to do *what?* He'd known they were dating, but the *Academy Awards!* That was something else entirely.

"Rhodes, I can't tell you what to do," he said finally. "But if you choose to go, you know what it will mean?"

"Um . . ." Rhodes chewed on his bottom lip, clearly at a loss as to what Page was getting at.

"It means coming out in public as her boyfriend, for one thing," he explained when Rhodes didn't say anything.

Rhodes frowned. "And that would be a bad thing?"

Page sighed. "No," he conceded. "But it's not just admitting publicly that you're together. It means giving up your privacy, grocery store tabloids, and the paparazzi shoving cameras in your face."

Rhodes shrugged. "We've had a few close calls with the paparazzi already, so their finding out about me is bound to happen sooner or later. But I don't think they'll find me very interesting after a few weeks. I mean, I come to work. I go home. I grocery shop. Not exactly tabloid fodder."

Page rubbed his eyes. He felt a headache coming on. "Then you're thinking about going with her." It was a statement, not a question.

"I—yes? But I don't know how the Bureau will feel about it."

Page leaned back in his chair. "Are you sure about this?" he asked, searching Rhodes's face.

Rhodes looked away, worrying at his bottom lip again. "I'm not sure about anything," he admitted finally, before looking back at Page again. "Except. Except that I think I'm falling in love with her." He shrugged helplessly. "And I don't want to have to sneak around to see her or hide it from anybody."

Page sighed. "In that case, we'll work it out," he said quietly. Even if it was a disaster in the making. He didn't know if Rhodes could handle it. He didn't know if the *Bureau* could handle it. Not to mention their Special Agent in Charge, Jayne Harbor. She was going to flip her lid over this.

Now there was a conversation he didn't want to have. He tapped a finger against his lips. Better to bypass her and go directly to their Assistant Director, he thought. Which was really going to piss her off, but she wasn't going to be his boss for very much longer, or Rhodes's for that matter either, although neither one of them knew that yet.

A relieved smile crossed Rhodes's face. "Thanks, Page," he said, getting up.

"There's just one more thing," Page added.

Rhodes turned back.

"You're going to need a tuxedo."

For a second Rhodes stared at him, bewildered. "I'll need a what?"

A rare smile crossed Page's face.

"Don't worry about it," he reassured him. "I've got a good tailor. We'll get you fitted out properly."

"A tux?" Rhodes said faintly.

"A tux," Page agreed.

"Can't I just—rent one?"

"No," Page said firmly. He was going to make sure Rhodes looked like a million bucks when he walked down the red carpet with Molly. And maybe, just maybe, they could keep the whole event from being a complete fiasco, too. He'd have to talk to their press liaison to see if they could find a way to manipulate the press before the awards show happened.

The short length of rebar had had a nice heft to it, which had been a bit of a surprise. It had been lighter than he'd expected too. One little swing, and he'd crushed the guy's skull in, tiny bits of bone and gore and brain matter exploding all over the place. Which had made a bit of a mess, but then, he wasn't the one who'd have to clean it up. And it wasn't like he'd planned on killing anyone, but the guy had been whistling tunelessly under his breath, on and on and on, like he was the only person in the universe.

He wasn't sure exactly when he'd had enough, but when the guy had gotten off the bus, he'd followed him. Down the street, then into the small alley parking lot that ran behind a row of businesses. He'd been close enough to hear him mutter, "Seriously, Jules?" as he'd stopped outside a door painted blue. A bag of trash leaned up against it, as if it had been forgotten on someone's way out. Grabbing up the bag, the guy had headed toward the dumpster at the end of the alley, taking up his tuneless, nails scrapping on a blackboard, whistling again from where he'd left off.

The rebar had simply been there, in a pile of other construction related debris and, whelp, the guy wasn't going to be whistling anymore. In tune, or out of it.

He tossed the rebar aside, a little sad to let it go. He'd liked it. Had liked the feel of it. Had liked how quickly it had taken the guy out, and the satisfying crunch it had made when it had connected. But it wasn't like he could stash a piece of it in his backpack. But . . . but a sap now, he thought, a sap would do the same thing, right? He'd have to look into getting one, or maybe, making one? It couldn't be that hard, right? And he did like a good DIY project.

He glanced around the alley, but he was still alone in it, which was a good thing, seeing as how it was the middle of the afternoon. Not to mention the fact it was kinda hard to miss the splayed-out dead body. Better yet, no cameras. A win-win situation all around.

Bending over, he scooped up the keys that had fallen from the dead man's hand, selecting the bright shiny one. Shiny was good. He didn't have a shiny one. Shiny meant new. He grinned. Not that this guy was going to be needing whatever new thing this key had gone to ever again. But . . . new was an interesting idea.

His eyes drifted to the rebar as he cocked his head and thought about it. Yes, new was a very good idea, and he didn't mean trying out a sap—although that was an excellent idea too. No, maybe, he needed to try somewhere *new. That could be fun. Maybe it was time to give the West Hollyweird PD a rest. See if, hmmm . . . He frowned for a minute, brows scrunching together again, then grinned. Maybe he'd see if the Beverly Hills PD were any better at their jobs than this useless lot were. They hadn't even begun to put two and two together yet. Duh. Hello? You have a serial killer in town. Idiots. But Beverly Hills with all its potential—oh yes, this was going to be so much fun!*

Whistling, he threw the key up into the air, catching it effortlessly as it tumbled back down again. Time to head home, dinner was cooking. A lovely chicken cacciatore in his Crock-Pot. Tomorrow, he'd start getting acquainted with his new hunting ground.

"Hey, Fount, get over here!" Gia called. Rhodes looked around from where he was fixing a cup of tea to see what was so urgent and noticed two things immediately: the first was that the members of his new team were in the conference room, staring at a large TV, and the second was that an anorexic entertainment reporter was talking animatedly on it.

"And here is Molly Whittier looking stunning in a pale blue Dior gown designed for tonight's Golden Globes appearance," she was saying excitedly as he walked in to join them, Page right on his heels. The office was empty behind them as the clock hands inched past eight p.m.

"Molly was due to arrive with her *Entangled* costar, Martin Riley," the reporter rushed on breathlessly, "but rumors are flying around the awards ceremony right now that the reason she's come with her brother is that she has a real-life beau and didn't want her fans to mistakenly think there was anything going on between herself and Riley. Let's see if we can't get a quick word with her."

"Molly! Molly is it true? Everyone wants to know—do you have a boyfriend?"

Molly smiled serenely. "Yes, it's quite true, and," she continued sincerely, "we would both like to thank the press for being so understanding in respecting our privacy."

"Oh, nice," said Romano, "who thought that one up?"

"Miranda," Page said grinning. He owed their press liaison a bouquet of flowers *and* chocolates for a job well done.

"Well," the reporter conceded, smiling a little bewilderedly, "we certainly respect your privacy."

"You will now," Talafiero said grinning.

"Thank you," Molly said gently, before moving away, the interview concluded gracefully.

"Nice," said Romano, "*very* nice." Raising his coffee mug in a toast toward Page, he added, "For manipulating the press so magnificently."

Page laughed. "You have no idea how much fun we had coming up with a way to leak 'the boyfriend' to the press," he told him.

"The boyfriend" put his head in his hands. "Why couldn't she have been a nice hairdresser or something?"

"A hairdresser!" Talafiero exclaimed. "A hairdresser would have run away screaming right after you said hello. Assuming you managed to *say* hello, that is."

"I don't know, Gia," Romano teased, "I've met a few smart,

sexy hairdressers, if I'd known that was what Rhodes was looking for—"

"All right, children," Page cut in firmly, "leave Rhodes alone."

"Yes, Dad," they chorused insincerely, and Rhodes groaned. He didn't mind their teasing, not really. It was what loomed ahead that terrified him. All those reporters, all those people. He swallowed hard. He could do this. He was an FBI agent for god's sake! He carried a gun and stared down bad guys every day. How hard could it be to stare down reporters?

"Fancy meeting you here!" Okay, that was a stupid thing to say, Tolliver berated himself, since it was a crime scene and May was the medical examiner.

She made a sound that was a cross between a giggle and a huff and said, "I could think of more romantic places for a first date."

Sully manfully turned his snort of laughter into a rib-jarring cough, then stepped away when Tolliver glared at him. Okay, so he didn't do smooth and debonair. "Me too," his mouth blurted out without consulting him first.

May paused in what she was doing and looked up at him and waited.

He froze like a deer in the headlights.

"Okay, then," she said finally and went back to examining

the body, while Tolliver desperately tried to think of some place to ask her out to.

"Uh, what if we try the first-date thing over dinner, instead of at a murder scene?" he came up with finally, proud of himself.

The snuffle laugh drifted up to him, before May cleared her throat and said, "That would be lovely."

"Great. Then it's a date."

"Just tell me when and where, and I'll be waiting."

EIGHT

MUCH ADO ABOUT NOTHING

Midterms sucked. Not to mention the fact that having to study for them was interfering with his plans for Beverly Hills. Then again, it wasn't like it was going anyplace. It would still be there in all its vain glory when the studying was done. He'd make up for lost time during Spring Break. But still, he thought he would have killed someone there by now, but, noooooo, school had to take precedent.

He glared at the open textbook in his lap before thinking, "fuck it," and slammed it shut. There were only so many mathematical principles you could cram into your head on an empty stomach.

Huh. He cocked his head as a thought drifted through his mind then took hold. What if he took a little study break and drove over to Beverly Hills, just for a quick look around?

It wasn't like he could afford to eat there. But he could afford a cup of joe at that coffee shop just off Rodeo Drive he'd been meaning to check out. And who knew, maybe their parking lot would be the perfect place for a nice stabbing. Hell, maybe he'd even take his knife along, you know, just in case. Because, why not? It would be a shame not to be prepared if an opportunity presented itself.

He dropped his math text on the coffee table, stood and stretched, before grabbing up his keys and heading out. He thought he might swing by that new Korean place on his way back. He had a taste for kimchi with maybe an order of bulgogi on the side. Yum.

"Sir? Can I talk to you a minute? It's about Rhodes," Page said as he stood in the doorway of the Assistant Director's office. Assistant Director John Franklin looked up, concern written large on his face. Page knew he had a special relationship with Rhodes, was in fact a family friend, and he was counting on that to secure his help with what he thought of as "the Academy Awards fiasco."

"Yes, of course. Is everything all right with Fountain?" he asked worriedly.

Page stepped into his office and closed the door.

"Everything's fine, sir," he reassured him quickly. "It's just he's about to do something that's going to thrust him into the public eye fairly spectacularly," and he went on to tell Franklin about Rhodes dating Molly.

"Molly Whittier, huh?" Franklin said, smiling slightly. "Well, good for him. So, what was the real reason you wanted to talk me?" And Page proceeded to tell him about the upcoming Academy Awards ceremony.

For a minute, Franklin sat deep in thought before saying, "We can deal with that. What else?"

"Special Agent in Charge Harbor," Page said quietly. His boss was going to blow a gasket when she found out about this. Which was one reason he was side stepping her and going directly to *her* boss.

"Ah." Franklin looked away for a moment, brows pulled together in thought before he looked back at Page and said, "I do believe that Judy and I will be hosting an Oscars' party this year, and I'm relatively certain Jayne won't want to miss it. Will that do, Page?"

"Yes, sir," Page agreed. That would do very nicely.

"So, what are you doing?" Molly's husky voice wrapped itself around Fountain, sliding into all his lonely nooks and crannies, tugging on his heart strings.

"Nothing," Fountain answered. He'd already done his laundry and vacuumed and was sprawled out on his couch. A muted hockey game he didn't care much about was playing on TV. He'd been contemplating mixing up a batch of chocolate chip cookies when she'd called. Comfort food for his aching heart, because he hated the fact that they were going to be apart for their first Valentine's Day tomorrow.

"Are you decent?"

He stared at his phone. What kind of question was that? "Um, yes?" he answered.

"Good. Then go open the front door."

What? Wait! "You're here?"

"Yeah," she laughed breathlessly.

Fountain didn't remember leaping over the arm of the couch or sprinting down the hallway. But he must have, because he didn't think he'd taken a single breath between the time she'd told him where she was and when he'd flung open the front door to find her standing there.

Snatching her up into his arms, he spun her around while peppering her face with soft kisses.

"I take it you missed me, then?" She laughed breathlessly once he set her down again.

"Every minute I'm not with you," he answered honestly.

Molly's eyes widened just a bit, and her breath hitched, before a huge smile crossed her face. "I miss you, too, you know." And at her words, his heart went thumpity thump.

"God I'm glad you're here," he laughed, stepping back to let her in.

"Well, you didn't think I was going to miss tomorrow, did you?" she asked, pulling off her coat before hanging it on a peg next to his.

"I just—I didn't want to ask if you could come," he said. "I thought you'd be up to your eyeballs in pre–Academy Award stuff."

"More like up to my eyeballs avoiding Ricki and all the

things she keeps trying to get me to do stuff," she answered, slipping into his arms again.

He pulled back a little so he could see her face.

"She doesn't know you're here, does she?" he asked, grinning.

"Nope. And it feels soooooo good to have snuck away!"

He couldn't help laughing. "I'm glad you snuck away, too."

"I wouldn't have missed our first Valentine's Day for the world."

"So, I thought we'd go to the Smithsonian and see the orchid exhibit first," she told him, leading the way down the hallway to the living room. Throwing herself down on the coach with a contented sigh, she continued, "Then we can find somewhere in D.C. to have a nice cozy lunch before maybe picking up some steaks with all the fixings to cook here so we don't miss any of the game?"

The game in question being the hockey game between the Washington Capitals and the Carolina Hurricanes.

"I even brought my Hurricanes shirt!" she added, beaming.

Dropping a kiss onto the tip of her nose, he slid onto the couch beside her, pulled her into his arms, and murmured, "That sounds perfect. All of it." Then time stood still as his lips found hers.

It was sometime later before he asked, "Do you want to go out for dinner or just order pizza in?"

"Oh god, I could kill for some pizza right now," she told him with a grin. "Ricki's terrified I'm going to gain a pound and not fit into my awards dress and has been shoving lettuce at me every chance she gets."

"Then pizza it is," Fountain said. "Do you want your own, or do you want to share?"

"And this is why you're the best boyfriend ever!" Molly said happily. "I'd like a small ham and pineapple, please."

Fountain blinked.

"What?" She asked worriedly. "Oh god, don't tell me you're one of those people who think that's sacrilege or something."

Fountain shook his head. "No. I think that's the perfect pizza. It's what I was going to order for myself."

"We should get married," she said, nodding emphatically. "We love the same hockey team, the same pizza, and you keep your house insanely clean. How is that?"

"Ah, well, I never know when a gorgeous woman might drop in on me," he answered, smiling.

"Goofball!"

"No! Seriously! My mom was here—unannounced—three days ago. Some kind of yarn thing at Fibre Space."

"Some kind of—what kind of yarn thing?" Molly demanded, sitting bolt upright and staring intently at him.

"Um. A trunk show?" Fountain said uncertainly, not entirely sure that was what it had been.

Grabbing up her phone from the coffee table where she'd tossed it earlier, Molly started frantically typing. "Oh my god,

Fount, it's this kick ass yarn from this dye shop in South Carolina and"—tap, tap, tap—"it's still here! And . . . they're going to be open tomorrow. Can we go?"

He thought she looked adorable, all wide eyed and hopeful.

"I have an idea. Let's go see the orchids, then come back here to Old Town for lunch somewhere. Then we can go to the yarn shop, and you can play to your hearts content."

"Yes! I'll even get some red yarn to knit you a nice winter scarf."

"Um, I'm not sure red is really my color."

"Pink then?" she teased.

He thought about it a minute before nodding. "Yeah, I can do pink."

"Pink it is, then. I'll see if I can find one with grey or black speckles in it, so it goes with your winter coat."

NINE

WHO IS HE?

He couldn't say what it was about the Academy Awards that excited him so much. It wasn't all the glitz and glitter, or all the beautiful people prancing around in their borrowed finery—he could care less about that. He tipped his head to the side as he watched a particularly annoying "star" gush about how talented her co-nominees were, while everyone knew how much she hated every last one of them. He hoped she lost; he really did. Hoped the camera zoomed in on her botoxed face when her name wasn't called. He wanted to see that split second where anger and humiliation met before she plastered an insincere smile on her lips.

He thought about killing her for a split second, but he didn't want to make her immortal. God knew her movies wouldn't. They were awful. All she'd ever been was a pretty face with good tits and a perky ass, and that bus had left the station a long time ago.

The camera shifted to show her husband, drunk already from the looks of it, and, oh, what fun, it had caught him ogling and flirting with some sweet young thing twenty years younger than his wife.

Maybe this was why he liked the Oscars so much, he thought. All the rage, the hate, the venomous sneers, the face lifts, the boob and butt jobs and the cheating, spread out like a glorious buffet to graze on.

And the fact that there was always something unexpected that happened. Something exciting. Something no one anticipated. He popped the top off another beer and settled back into his couch to wait for it. Whatever "it"' was.

The black SUV waited only long enough for its passenger to get his bag out of the back before it sped away down the quiet street, leaving Rhodes staring anxiously at the sprawling beach house in front of him.

Swallowing hard, he pressed the bell only to have the door open practically immediately. A slender man with elaborately coiffed blond hair stood in the entrance, smiling pleasantly.

"Dr. Rhodes?" he asked.

Rhodes nodded, suddenly feeling completely out of his element. "Um, yeah, I am."

"Welcome. I'm Jonathon Freem, Molly's housekeeper, stylist, confidant, and personal assistant slash gofer," he added, smiling.

Rhodes nodded. He knew who Jonathon was, in theory at

least. But now, standing here face to face with the man, suddenly the whole Academy Awards thing wasn't a dream—it was really happening.

"Molly said you were gorgeous, but I think she missed the mark by a country mile," Freem said, his small welcoming smile changing to a much broader one as his gaze took Rhodes in from stem to stern.

She had?

"You're definitely something I can work with," he added. "Now, we're a little pushed for time, so," he continued, hurrying Fountain through the main part of the house, down a hallway and into an enormous guest bedroom, "I'm going to suggest you take a quick shower while I press your clothes. There's a private bath right though there. And Dr. Rhodes, please don't shave. I'll do that for you."

For a minute, Rhodes just stood there, completely over-whelmed, a million questions on his tongue, but Freem had already turned away and was taking his tuxedo out of his bag and making tsking noises over the creases in it. Suddenly the man looked up and said, "Well, what are you still doing here? Go!" and Rhodes went, relieved in some small way to simply be following orders.

He'd just finished dressing when Freem walked back into the guest room. He felt awkward in the white shirt and black trousers and had no idea how to tie the weird tie. Freem paused, studying him.

"What?" Rhodes asked, made uncomfortable by the man's intense stare.

"Undo your top button," he ordered. "Hmmm, better. Now, ditch the tie."

God yes, gladly, Rhodes thought, tossing the slip of a black ribbon onto the bed behind him.

Freem tipped his head to the side, a frown making a crease between his pale blue eyes. "You were wearing a purple tie when you got here," he murmured to himself, before rummaging through Rhodes's clothes again. "Ah ha! Here, put it back on."

Rhodes did as he was told completely bewildered.

"Not so tight!" Freem yelled suddenly, scaring Rhodes half to death. "It needs to *complement* the unbuttoned collar . . . Yes, like that. Much better!

"Yes," Freem said, nodding his head in satisfaction. "Yesssss. Now just slip on your jacket, and we'll—oh my." He stopped talking when Rhodes slipped on the new black shoulder holster Page had made him buy, checked the load in his gun, and holstered it.

"What?" Rhodes asked, alarmed by the look on Freem's face.

Freem gestured at Rhodes's weapon, "You," he gulped. "You're going to wear that?"

Rhodes nodded. "Yes." He always wore it.

"Oh," Freem breathed. Then he took a deep breath and squeaked, "Well, let's see how it looks with the jacket on." And as Rhodes slipped the specially tailored tuxedo jacket on and settled it into place, Freem said, "Oh my. You have an excellent tailor, Dr. Rhodes. You can't tell you're wearing a weapon at all."

Which was a good thing, Rhodes thought, because he was pretty sure the tuxedo hadn't been cheap. But he didn't actually know, since Page hadn't let him pay for it. It was a gift, he'd told him, from the whole team.

Freem's head tilted to the side again. "Hmmm. We're still missing something." He poked around in Rhodes's bag again before he stood up, smiling, a purple scarf in his hands. He flung it carelessly around Rhodes's neck and said, "There. Yes. Perfect."

"Now, just slip your jacket off for a minute, I'm going to trim your five o'clock shadow, but I think we need to leave most of it, so pay attention, that way next time you can do it yourself."

Next time. Fountain swallowed hard, suddenly realizing that there was going to be a next time, and a time after that too, for as long as he and Molly were together. Tuxedo suits and paparazzi and people like Jonathon fussing over him and, he suddenly realized, he could live with all of it to be with Molly.

When he was finished, Freem beamed at him, practically bouncing in place. "Yes," he said nodding, "I do believe, that when the night is over, the most talked about item at this year's Oscar's will be you and Molly."

Oh god, Rhodes thought, he hoped not.

"Don't even *think* about touching her!" Freem squeaked a few minutes later as Fountain stared awestruck at Molly. She was stunning, dressed in a shimmering gold, off the shoulder dress that swirled around her feet. Her hair had been pinned up in a tumble of curls that cascaded down her back like frothy waves.

"Molly you look beyond beautiful," he breathed.

"And you, Dr. Rhodes, look very gorgeous, yourself," she told him, her beautiful blue eyes bright with excitement. "You look both suave and sexy and dear god, good enough to eat," she added, her husky voice just a little breathless, and Rhodes could feel the hot blush that burned across his cheeks.

"All right, children, eyes on me please," Fremm interrupted. "There are just a few things we need to run through briefly." He waited a second before continuing. "Now, in order to protect your privacy as much as possible once tonight is through, we are going for the classic movie-star aura, 'look but don't intrude.'

"So, you may hold hands," he went on briskly, "and you, Dr. Rhodes, when you stop to acknowledge the crowds or pause to have your pictures taken, may put your arm around her and place your hand at her waist. Molly, you may lay a hand on his arm, but that is as much touching as I wish to see. Think Grace Kelly and Cary Grant."

Fountain could feel his heart racing. He wasn't ready to do this. He was as far from Cary Grant as you get, and he'd probably trip over his own feet and knock Molly down. Suave, he wasn't.

"A bulletin will be issued to the press as you walk down the

red carpet revealing your identity, Dr. Rhodes," Fremm
continued.

Extra! Extra! Batman is really Bruce Wayne. Rhodes could
see the headline clearly.

"So, by the time you're in the interview area, everyone is
going to know you're an FBI agent," Fremm went on calmly. "I
know your press liaison has briefed you on what you may and
may not say, so keep to your script. Be charming, be gracious,
and be brief. You'll be fine," he added, as if he knew the
thoughts that were racing through Fountain's mind.

"Now, the car is here. Dr. Rhodes, please don't forget to
breathe," he added dryly.

The team was gathered in Page's spacious living room, enjoying
the fine food and drinks their host had provided. The huge TV
tuned to the awards show. They were having a good time
commenting on all the stars as they arrived and made their way
down the infamous red carpet, waiting for Rhodes's "moment of
doom," as they'd dubbed it.

In an even larger living room, in a different part of town, a
different group had gathered to watch the awards show. Alcohol
flowed freely and every now and again John Franklin and his
wife, Judy, shared a private smile as they waited for a certain
young couple to arrive at the famous Kodak Theatre.

. . .

"We're awaiting the arrival of Molly Whittier, who recently set the entertainment world on its ear by admitting to having a mystery boyfriend."

The cameras cut away from the commentator as a limo pulled up. For a moment the doorway remained empty before a tall, slender young man got out. The DD nudged his wife's arm.

"Oh my god," the commentator breathed, "I do not know who that is, but he is gorgeous! Mark, find out who—" Her voice trailed off as a radiant Molly Whittier got out of the limo after him. For just a second, they stood smiling at each other before he twined his fingers in hers and they turned to face the crowds that lined the walkway.

"Oh my god!" echoed Gia, stunned, as Rhodes stepped out of the limo. Somehow, he'd been transformed from the worst dressed man in the history of planet earth to the sexy, gorgeous man on the screen.

Page and Romano exchanged a grin.

Across town, Special Agent in Charge Harbor stared, open mouthed in horror, at the screen. "No! That cannot be *Rhodes?*" She took a quick fortifying gulp of her drink before saying, "John, I had no idea—"

"It's fine, Jayne. I did," he said biting back a smile as Harbor's expression went from horrified to furious as she realized *someone* had sought permission for this *by going over her head.*

"Rhodes?" echoed Judy, "you don't mean that *that's* Dr. Fountain Rhodes?" she asked coyly, as if she hadn't known him for years. "Oh my." She fanned herself. "Jayne, how on earth do you get anything done with *that* to look at all day!"

Franklin laughed. "They certainly make a nice couple," he said, as if the fact that one of his best agents strolling down the red carpet at the Academy Awards with a gorgeous movie star on his arm was something that happened every day. And then he squeezed his wife's hand and kissed her on the cheek. God, he loved this woman.

Meanwhile, back at the awards ceremony, the almost hysterical commentator bellowed again, "Mark, find out who he is!"

Rhodes and Molly walked slowly down the carpet, smiling at the fans. Molly waved with one hand while keeping her other one tightly entwined in Rhodes's. Halfway down the carpet, they paused, and he slipped an arm around her waist, looking for all the world as if he did photo ops every day, then they walked on, hand in hand again.

"Mark!" The announcer was almost weeping in frustration. "Find me something—"

"We've just received a bulletin from the Federal Bureau of Investigation," a voice cut into the live feed. "It seems Ms. Whittier's boyfriend is FBI Special Agent Dr. Fountain Rhodes. He's thirty years old, and according to the press release, he's a psychiatrist currently attached to the Criminal Investigations Division in Manassas, Virginia."

In Franklin's living room, Special Agent in Charge Harbor

poured herself another drink.

In Page's living room a cheer went up at the announcement.

On the red carpet, Dr. Fountain Rhodes looked a little surprised when someone holding up a cell phone yelled out, "I love you, Dr. Rhodes!" and then he laughed as Molly said something to him privately.

———

And in a suburb not far away from all the evening's hoopla, a young man leaned forward as he stared at his TV. Whoa, that was the same Fed who'd given those lectures MurderDude had posted online last year. He was sure of it. How cool—and weird—was that? And unexpected. Huh, he'd thought Molly Whittier was dating her costar, Martin Riley. That's what the tabloids said. A little grin tugged at his lip before turning into a full-blown laugh. But he couldn't help it. How humiliating was that, being dumped for a Fed! He bet Riley was one royally pissed-off dude, especially now that everyone knew about it.

Leaning back in his overstuffed armchair, he stared up at the ceiling and savored the thought for another minute before his mind circled back around to the fact Molly Whittier's new love interest was a Fed.

Huh. The FBI, he mused thoughtfully, looking back at the couple on the screen again. Now that might be a game worth playing. But how to draw them in? How—oh yes. An idea flitted through his head. That would be perfect! Perfect indeed and so much fun to implement!

TEN
WHY ME?
EARLY MARCH

Asshole! Who did he think he was, cutting him off like that, making him jump back that way? Pedestrians had the right of way, right? You couldn't just drive over them pulling into a parking space. And it wasn't like the asshole couldn't see him. There were fucking lights in the alley!

Okay, so maybe he'd technically stepped out in front of the car, but it wasn't like he'd known it was trying to pull into *a space. He'd been watching the cars that were already parked, trying not to get run over by any that were leaving, thinking about which site he wanted to use for his first kill in Beverly Hills, since he'd struck out with the first location. He* hadn't *been watching for assholes who were trying to park.*

The guy hadn't even bothered to use his indicator to let him know what he was doing, either. Asshole. He wasn't a frickin' mind reader. How was he supposed to know the guy wanted to drive right over the top of where he was walking? It wasn't like he'd *been about to take the parking space. What did the guy think he was going to do, lay down in it?*

And now the guy was laughing at him. Really funny. Ha, ha, ha. He could have been hurt! Killed even . . . He bet the asshat wouldn't be laughing quite so hard when he stuck a gun in his face.

"So, it really wasn't as bad as you thought it would be, was it?" Molly teased, leaning back in Fountain's arms to see his face. It had been twelve days since he'd last seen her. Twelve days since the awards ceremony, and Fountain still wasn't sure he'd recovered from it completely.

He dropped a kiss on her nose, thinking, no, it had been infinitely worse. He hadn't known about the six after parties, or the early morning breakfast they'd had to go to. In comparison, the awards show had been a breeze.

Curled up in each other's arms on his couch, a warm afternoon breeze drifting idly through the open French doors, Fountain was still trying to decide what had been the weirdest part of the whole thing.

"It was . . . different," he settled on finally, and when she dissolved into laughter against his chest, he found himself grinning along with her, after a bit.

The number of people who had wanted to talk to him had been—overwhelming. Directors, producers, movie stars, all wanting to ask him things just because he was a *real* Federal Agent.

Did he want to consult on their next great hit—Um, no. Were they crazy?

Or—god forbid—help write it, so it was more authentic?

Although his personal favorite had been from some "A" lister who wanted to know if he could "ride shotgun"—whatever that meant, since Fountain usually "rode a desk"—on Fountain's next case so he could *feel* his next role more fully . . . God, was that even a thing? And had the guy really expected him to say yes?

Then there had been the questions he'd expected: had he ever shot someone? Had he ever interviewed any of the really famous serial killers? And then the one he hadn't understood at all: Was he part of the conspiracy to keep the people downtrodden? He'd had no idea what that one even meant.

He'd been rescued from answering by a country music star who, after draping herself all over him, had wanted to know if he was "available." Which had sent Molly into a fit of giggles and had spurred him into taking her home. Enough was enough.

Especially since he'd had to be on a plane just a few short hours later.

Snuggling closer, Molly pulled his head down towards her and just before their lips met said, "I thought you were very brave. Thank you for coming with me."

Sergeant Alejandro Sullivan hurried down the hall toward the break room where he was pretty sure his boss had just gone to snag another cup of coffee. Or at least that was where he hoped the man was, and not halfway home already. It was bad enough that they'd both wound up working late, but he didn't want to be the one to have to call Tolliver back and tell him their day was about to get even longer. Dead bodies had a way of doing that. And they definitely had another dead body.

Poking his head in through the break-room door, Sully sighed. Tolliver's back was to him, but from where he stood, he could clearly see his boss stirring his coffee. And stirring and stirring and—which just went to tell him how tired his boss really was since the man took his coffee black . . .

"Sir?" he called softly. "We've had a shooting. A Patrick Howell, shot once in the face in his car. He was found by the guy parked next to him."

And this is what happened when you stayed late, Tolliver thought tiredly, staring at the spoon he was stirring his coffee with. Which was weird, since he didn't take milk or sugar. Taking the spoon out of his mug and setting it aside, he took a sip. No point wasting it, and the way this evening was setting up, he was going to need all the coffee he could get.

"Where? No, let me guess. West Hollywood?" And at Sully's nod, he thought, what the hell was going on? This was the third killing in West Hollywood since January. If he didn't know better, he'd think they were connected. But they couldn't be, could they? He shook his head. No. He was just being stupid, and frustrated, since he wasn't having any luck solving the first two and now he'd caught another one.

Still, on the bright side, it meant he'd get to see May, and he'd finally figured out where he wanted to take her on their first date. Dinner and dancing at that new place by the pier.

ELEVEN

FUN & GAMES

APRIL FOOL'S DAY

He smiled. He was just that smart, and they were just that dumb. Look at them, each one so sure of his own importance that they were ruining the crime scene, tramping through it on their way to take a look at the empty, lifeless carcass he'd left for them. God, this was perfect, better than the circus!

He'd seen one, once, years ago. His dad had taken him. The best part had been when a trapeze artist had fallen to his death right in front of them. He'd laughed out loud and clapped his hands at the crumpled bloody wreck of a man, neck broken, head a gory mess, eyes staring sightlessly right at him. His dad had squeezed him on the shoulder, gently. Dear old Dad, he'd understood the rush he'd felt, completely.

He flexed his fingers and looked around. So many gawkers, yesssss! He looked back at the cops. Ah, what a comedy! Now the detectives were arguing over jurisdiction, since this particular alley butted up against the border line between Beverly Hills and West

Hollywood. He'd done it on purpose, of course, killed here, just to watch them. They were so damn easy to manipulate. So predictable, unlike him.

He hadn't fallen into the "serial killer trap," as he fondly liked to think of it. He didn't really care who the victim was; it was more about desire. When the desire hit, he simply acted on it. And as for a weapon, this time he'd tried his new homemade, lead-filled sap, and it had been perfect. It had crushed her head in without spreading her brains about. A quick step up behind her as she headed for her car and BAM! She'd gone down without so much as a whimper.

He pushed his hands deeper into his pockets and fingered the car fob he'd removed from the woman's hand. It hadn't taken long for someone to find her. Just long enough for him to get a coffee around the corner. He'd waited inside while the cop cars had raced by, lights and sirens blaring, then had given it a little longer for a crowd to gather and for the pissing match between the two sets of detectives to begin.

He shivered slightly as a gust of wind found him. Damn, it was getting chilly now that night was falling, the cold front finally blowing in, just like the weatherman had said. Ah well, no point standing around any longer and getting chilled to the bone. He'd seen enough. He might as well go home and fix something good for dinner. Maybe a beef Wellington with new potatoes and baby green beans on the side, and a nice chocolate soufflé for dessert? Yes, that sounded about right, and Dad would enjoy it.

"Sir?" Sullivan's voice sounded strained as it slid out of the speaker on Tolliver's cell phone. Considering it was seven o'clock at night, he should have sounded pissed off too, Tolliver thought, seeing as how their shift was long over, so a call at this hour didn't bode well for either one of them. In the background, Tolliver heard a car horn blaring, which meant Sully was already on his way to pick him up so they could get to wherever it was they were going.

Damn it all. He'd only just popped the top off a cold one and pulled his dinner out of the oven.

"Sir?"

Tolliver grunted irritably in reply. Something between a "yeah?" and a "what now?"

"West Hollywood just called in a homicide. White female, head crushed in. Victim was found lying beside her car about half an hour ago."

"Let me guess, in an alley." Tolliver rubbed his eyes at Sully's apologetic sigh. "And we're being called in why, exactly?"

"Because there's a jurisdictional squabble going on with Beverly Hills PD. Seems like the alley is literally the boundary between the two cities."

"So why doesn't West Hollywood let them have it?"

Sully snorted. "Because they were the first to respond."

Ah—geez. Just lovely. "Fine, let's go take a look, see what's what. But I'm telling you, Sully," he added, covering his dinner with aluminum foil before putting it in his refrigerator for later, "I'm starting to get a bad feeling about all these murders. Four homicides in West Hollywood in three, no four months just this year alone? Not to mention the unsolved ones from last year." He shook his head. A *really* bad feeling.

He still thought the same thing three days later. Especially after May made the comment that you didn't see too many people with their heads smashed in. They'd looked into that, of course, but had come up empty. Still, there was just something about these murders, about all of them, that was nagging at him. Something he couldn't quite put his finger on. But he knew who might. He hated bringing in the Feds, but he didn't know what else to do.

TWELVE

SMITH & WESSON

He caught a snatch of a popular song as he passed by an open dorm-room window, trudging his way between classes. Something about love gone wrong and walking away from it because who needed love, anyway?

The words tore something loose inside him. Not about love, because, yeah, who did need that, right? But about something else he hadn't realized had been lurking in the back of his mind until now.

"Used to love you, but now I hate you . . ."

Which pretty much summed up what he'd been feeling about his major lately. Did he really need a college degree in mathematics? It wasn't like he was ever going to use it, and, according to Professor Stone, he was crappy at it anyway. Not to mention the fact that it wasn't particularly useful when it came to killing people. Now if they'd offered a BA in serial killing, he'd have been all over it. Or would it be a BS, he mused? He grinned at the thought of it. It really should be a major. The classes would be packed. And, it would be so much more useful than— He came to a shambling stop.

Wait. Why exactly was he wasting his time doing something he'd grown to hate? He cocked his head, thinking about it, then a smile spread very slowly across his face as he realized there was no reason at all for it, and suddenly, he felt just so much better. Like an enormous weight had been lifted from his shoulders. He should really thank Professor Stone for helping him to see the error of his ways. It was only fair.

Yes, he decided. He'd thank her properly, then drop out, especially as he didn't really have time right now for his classes, anyway. He wasn't entirely sure how his dad would feel about it, but a nice dinner should take care of that. Comfort food. Like meatloaf and mashed potatoes with peas. He nodded to himself, perfect. And maybe a nice bubbly to celebrate his liberation from the halls of academia. After all, champagne went with everything, right?

Wes Smith, whose real name was John, walked across the conference room to where his new partner was contemplating a series of papers pinned to the wall in front of him.

"So, what are we looking at?" he asked, coming to a stop beside the man he hadn't met yet.

Wes was a big, heavily muscled man, with broad shoulders, cornflower blue eyes, and blond hair, which for reasons he'd never understood, was lighter on the top than the sides.

"Not sure, exactly," Fountain replied, without taking his gaze from the grisly photographs he was staring at so intently. "A Detective Tolliver, from the L.A. County Sheriff's Department made an inquiry to the local Bureau office, asking if they'd take a look at a string of unusual murders in West Hollywood. But they've got their hands full doing something else and passed it on to us. So, that's what we're doing. Looking," he added, sounding oddly cheerful at the thought of it.

Wes slid a sideways glance at the man. Yup, definitely happy, and when he started humming the soundtrack to *The Little Shop of Horrors* softly to himself, Wes had to bite back a snort of amusement. He'd been told Rhodes was a little different when he'd asked around, but he had a feeling different might not begin to cover it.

"So, how unusual are we talking about?" he asked. Because while he might not know much about Fountain Rhodes, except for what he'd read in the grocery-store tabloid headlines, he did know Detective Tolliver. And for the man to have reached out to the Feds meant something about these murders had him more than a little worried.

"In January, Mary Fiennes was stabbed with a knitting needle in the alley parking lot beside a local coffee shop where her knit group meets regularly," Rhodes told him without any preamble, pointing a long slender finger at the first crime scene photograph.

A knitting needle? Okay. Yeah, that definitely went into the unusual category.

"Jaquille Shonte was hit over the head with a piece of rebar while taking the trash out behind his business, also in January," Rhodes continued. "While Patrick Howell was found slumped over the wheel of his car, shot once in the face in March. And just last week, Inez Park was found with her skull smashed in."

"And let me guess," Wes interrupted, "the last two were also in alley parking lots."

"Yes!" Rhodes agreed so enthusiastically Wes had to bite the inside of his cheek to keep from grinning. God, his new partner was a trip.

But the graphic pictures in front of him were not, and while getting killed in parking lots, whether they were alleys or not, wasn't unusual, Wes had to agree with Tolliver that something seemed to be going on in West Hollywood. It could be coincidence, or it could be something else. Staring at the photographs, he knew what it was that was niggling at him.

"Feels a little bit like a baby serial killer, just trying out his wings," Wes said thoughtfully. And put that way, the alleys screamed that they were all connected, even if the methods were wildly different.

"Right?" Rhodes agreed, practically bouncing on his toes, his eyes sparkling as he looked at Wes for the first time, clearly relieved that Wes had come to the same conclusion that he had.

"So, where do you want to begin?" Wes asked, gesturing at the stacks of folders representing the victims' lives piled on the conference table behind them.

"By introducing myself?" his new partner said with a sheepish grin. "Fountain Rhodes," he added, offering a hand.

"John Smith, though most people call me Wes."

A confused expression crossed his new partner's face before he got it. "Oh! Smith and Wesson!" He laughed, clearly delighted at the cleverness of it. "How appropriate," he added, then with one final snort of amusement, his eyes drifted back to the papers beside them. "I'll take numbers if you'll take words," he suggested, his mind already focusing back on the job in front of them. "Romano and Talafiero are running down credit cards and phone records."

Good, Wes thought, having met the two other team members of the newly formed Special Investigation's Unit just a few minutes before he'd tracked Rhodes down in the conference room. Going through people's lives took time, and the more people working on it, the faster they'd reach a conclusion as to whether or not the murders were connected.

"Oh!" Rhodes suddenly exclaimed, a touch of color staining his cheeks, looking up from the stack of files he'd pulled toward himself, as if he'd just remembered something important he'd forgotten to say. "And um, maybe we could get a beer or dinner sometime soon? With Gia and Nico. You know, to get to know each other, seeing as how this is all new. Working together. As a team. And, um, as partners?" he added awkwardly, before simply stopping as if he didn't know either how or if he should keep on going.

"Sounds like a plan," Wes agreed, hiding a smile as he

dragged a stack of folders toward himself and sat down, adding socially awkward to his list of things he was learning about his partner.

"Great." Rhodes nodded, a smile sliding across his face, before his eyes drifted down to the papers in front of him, and within seconds, he'd pulled out a chair of his own and had become completely engrossed in his work. A welcome salvation, Wes thought, from having to converse.

Well, if nothing else, Wes knew that having Fountain Rhodes as a partner was never going to be dull. Quirky and odd maybe, but never dull. And he would need to bring his "A" game if he wanted to keep up with him. Quirky and odd, he knew, tended to equal brilliant, and he had a feeling that Dr. Fountain Rhodes was smarter than most.

———————

Guns were loud and messy, he thought, not for the first time, looking down at the body sprawled across the concrete of the parking garage floor. Bits of bone and brain matter fanned out across the wall behind where the woman had been standing when he'd called out to her. She'd turned, of course, recognizing his voice, and he'd shot her. Who'd known there'd be such a mess after?

Huh, okay, so the parking-lot dude's brains had spattered everywhere, too. Unlike that family he'd shot. So, these bullets weren't as good as the other ones he'd used. Those ones hadn't made a mess at all. Interesting.

It wasn't just the gore on the wall, either. A pool of blood was forming beneath what remained of her head, black in the garage's poor lighting, but curiously a bright, almost neon, red where it was soaking into the papers that had scattered around Professor Stone when she'd fallen.

One of them caught his eye. It had his name on it, a red "A" in the top right-hand corner, and rightly so. He'd worked his butt off for it. But not anymore. He was done with school now, and the decision was like being reborn. No more pressure, no more tests, no more exams. No more petty people acting as if they had something to teach him. Something *important he had to learn to unlock the meaning of the universe.*

Yeah, well, he already had that part down pat. You lived, then you died. Sometimes with a bullet in your brain. He stared down at the lifeless woman at his feet, noting for the first time the butterfly tattooed just above her right knee, and couldn't help grinning. Fly away, Professor. See? I've set us both free.

Free. He looked around the still empty parking deck and nodded. Time to leave. He cocked his head, trying to hear if there were anyone else around. Anyone calling out. But his ears were still ringing from the concussion of sound the gun shot had created. He hadn't realized how it would bounce off the walls and amplify into such a grand crescendo, a finale of such towering magnitude. It wasn't like that had happened when he'd fired the gun before at what's her name's house, or in the alley when he'd shot asshole parking dude. Whelp. Now he knew.

Bending down, he scooped up the woman's office door key from the ground. Thank god it hadn't fallen into the blood and gore. That would have been disgusting. And how nice of her to have had it ready and waiting in her hand when she'd gotten out of her car, laden down with her papers and laptop. Saved him from having to look for it. He slipped it into his pocket, then stuffed the gun back into his backpack.

Then with one last glance around, he walked away, clattering down the stairwell and out into the bright sunlight heralding the start to another fine day. His stomach growled, ready for breakfast. An omelet maybe? With potatoes and onions and green peppers and —it was amazing how killing made him so hungry. He needed to remember that next time and pack a snack.

The best part about having a key collection was no one noticed it. They might glance at it and think, "Well, that's different." But they didn't go from, "Huh he collects keys," to, "He must be a serial killer." No, keys were the perfect trophy. A person missing a key was, well, just a person missing a key, unlike a person missing a body part. Now there was a sure-fire way to alert the police that they had a wacko running around the place. Really, some people were such idiots. But a key, now that was pure genius. He doubted the police would ever make that connection.

He stroked the key he was currently holding and smiled fondly at it before hanging it up in the very last slot in his current display box. He'd need to remember to get a new box in the morning.

"So, how did it go?" Molly asked, still wrapped up in the "hello" hug Fountain had enveloped her in when he'd gotten home, the taste of him lingering on her lips from his kiss. And god, the man could kiss. She thought that was what she missed the most when they weren't together. His kisses, and the feeling of utter peace she had when she was near him. The minute he wrapped his arms around her, all the stress of the day, all the worries and tension, fell away.

She'd stolen four days to come be with him. Four days away from the nonsense that was Hollywood. Four days to just be Molly to his Fountain. She burrowed deeper into his arms, inhaling the clean, crisp scent of the man, never wanting to let go of him. She didn't want to have to leave tomorrow. She hadn't had enough time with him yet, *damn it.*

Loosening his arms just a little, Fountain leaned back so he could see her better.

"How did what go?" he asked, clearly confused and a little worried that he'd forgotten to do something.

She kissed the corner of his mouth in reassurance, loving the taste of him. A little citrusy, a little sweet, as if he'd had a little piece of orange chocolate on his way home from work. Which, knowing him, he probably had. "How did meeting your new partner go?" she asked, smiling just a little. God, she loved this dear, sweet, awkward man.

"Oh!" His brow unfurrowed, relief clear on his face. "Good. Yes." He nodded as if that covered everything.

Twining their fingers together, she chuckled to herself as she led him deeper into the house. "So, what's he like?" she asked, knowing she'd have to ask to find out anything about the man.

Tossing his jacket and tie on the back of a kitchen chair, before drifting on to the den to lock his gun in the cleverly disguised end-table safe, he took his time thinking his answer through. It gave her plenty of time to grab a couple of IPAs before joining him.

"Big. And, um, blond," he said finally, settling down into the big squishy couch that faced the French doors to the garden and gratefully taking the IPA she handed him.

"Not my type then," Molly teased, curling up beside him and tugging on his unruly brown hair.

"Oh, I don't know," Fountain said, the hint of a smile on his lips. "You like smart men, and he is. Very."

"Well, that's a relief," she teased, "not that Page would have picked anyone stupid for his first command, or as your partner." She raised her own bottle of beer and said, "To Thomas Page, Special Agent in Charge of the brand-new Special Investigations Unit! God, what a mouthful!"

Clinking their bottles together, Fountain said, "I'll drink to that." Having Page as his boss was so much better than having Harbor, and the new unit would be—interesting.

"Thought you might," Molly said, before adding, "And, speaking of smart men, Michael called earlier."

Fountain smiled. "Everything good with the professor?" he

asked. Using his nickname for her brother. They'd become good friends over the winter vacation.

"No, not really," she admitted, a hint of sadness in her voice, which got his attention. "A colleague of his, a friend, was murdered this morning on campus."

Fountain blinked, shocked. "What! Who?" Oh god, he probably knew the victim. He'd gone to CalTech before going on to Stanford to do his doctorate and go to med school. Not that Michael had been teaching at CalTech when he'd been there.

"Professor Stone. Someone shot her as she was getting out of her car."

"Stone?" He swallowed hard. "Anna Stone? I took classes with her," he half whispered, stunned, before peppering Molly with rapid-fire questions. "Do they know who did it? Did they catch the guy? Do they have any witnesses?"

"No, they don't have any idea who did it. No one saw anything. It was really early, and the cameras in the parking garage had been spray painted over. Someone's been spraying them all over campus."

He couldn't believe it. Who would want to kill Professor Stone?

"Michael must be beside himself. Maybe I should give him a call? I mean, I'm assuming they closed campus down, at least for today, right, and that he's gone home?"

Home to the house he shared with Molly and their housekeeper, so at least he wouldn't be alone.

She nodded. "Yes, they closed it, and yes, he went home.

He's pretty much wrecked. But last time I talked to him, Jonathon was planning on making him a cup of hot tea with honey and bourbon, then tucking him into bed."

Which sounded like a sensible plan to Fountain. But then Jonathon was a very sensible man, and a first-class housekeeper, valet, stylist, and friend. Michael was in good hands. He'd make some calls tomorrow to see if the police had found out anything, and then he'd call him. Damn. He couldn't believe it. Who would want to kill Anna Stone?

Rolling his shoulders to loosen his muscles, Wes leaned back in his chair and let his eyes drift over to his partner, who was peering at the white board in front of him again as if he might find the answers to the universe in the grisly photographs taped to it. Or at least, some kind of an answer as to whether or not the killings were connected. And he probably would, Wes mused. The man saw patterns where there were none for mere mortals to see.

Pity he couldn't see them when he got dressed in the morning. Wes stifled a snort. Simply put, in the few weeks since he'd started working with the man, he'd determined that Fountain Rhodes was quite possibly the worst-dressed person he'd ever met. His bizarre array of vests and ties had become an almost constant source of amusement for Wes. So much so that he'd started a "Rhodes Lottery" at the office centered on which awful vest or tie the man would be wearing on any given day.

Today, Rhodes had managed to pair a teal vest with the dark gray charcoal suit he was wearing, and, as an added bonus in the lottery, he had outdone himself by adding a red tie with giant white flowers splashed over it, winning Wes a hundred dollars. For a moment, Wes wondered how he got away with ignoring the Bureau's dress code when it came to his ties, before deciding that in the interest of solving cases, the higher ups could probably care less what the man wore, as long as he was solving cases.

Rhodes also, on occasion, showed up for work dressed in corduroy pants and tweed jackets—the Bureau having discovered early on that people opened up to him when he was dressed like that. Useful in interrogations. His nonthreatening air and quiet manner caused people to simply tell him things they wouldn't have told another agent. Besides, no one really believed he was a Federal Agent when he was dressed like that.

Not that Wes was the most fashion-conscious guy himself. He had a variety of gray and black suits with shirts and ties that went with all of them, no matter the combination, to wear at work. Outside of work, he stuck to jeans and simple T-shirts with an occasional sweatshirt when the weather got colder. Idly, he wondered if Rhodes would go psychotic if he snuck into his home and removed the worst of his offending ties. And vests, too, for that matter. He shuddered, despite himself. The man might be brilliant when it came to finding patterns, but he was most definitely not a fashion plate.

Although, now that he thought about it, when they'd first met, Rhodes's wardrobe had seemed more put together. Something his girlfriend had had a hand in? Had she been in town visiting him? He'd have to ask Gia if she'd noticed or knew.

Right on cue, Gia Talafiero pushed open the door to the conference room and dumped a new stack of papers next to the others that were already on the table. More information on the lives of the murder victims.

"Find anything?" Wes asked.

"Nope, these people's paths did not cross. Different doctors, lawyers, banks, churches, kids' schools, kids' sports, their own interests, their grocery stores, orthodontists, eye doctors, dry cleaners."

"Sex clubs?"

Wes and Gia stared at Rhodes like he'd grown a third head, skipping right past a second one.

"Say what?" Gia managed.

"Sex clubs." Rhodes repeated, turning to look at them. Face serious.

"Uh." Gia shook her head. "You know something we don't, Fount?"

"No. But it wasn't on your list."

Casting a "do not mess with me" look at Wes, she said, "I'll get right on that." Which was met with a huge smile by Fountain, obviously happy that he'd thought of something no one else had.

Wes had to bite his tongue to keep from laughing. God, he loved working with this man who, he was learning, saw the world so differently than most other people did. Not that Wes saw the world strictly in black and white, but he didn't see the shadows and bursts of sunlight like his new partner did. Wes was more of an oak who stood against the wind, while Fountain Rhodes *was* the wind, picking up ideas and tossing them aside from the facts and figures other people handed him.

Now if they could just give the man enough information to determine whether or not West Hollywood had a serial killer on the loose. Or if the murders were just that: murders, unconnected in any way.

Out in the bull pen, he could see Gia at a computer— looking into sex clubs, he supposed, biting back a snort. As if these people had been secret swingers. He shook his head, wishing he knew where Rhodes pulled his thoughts from. Sex clubs? Really?

At the desk next to Gia, her partner, Nico Romano was on the phone. He'd been sifting through credit card charges. But the dead had not had so much as a single charge at even the same gas station as far as they'd been able to determine.

The door opened again, and this time it was Roxy Greene who sailed through it—the newest addition to their team. She'd been compiling all the forensic evidence.

Wes smiled. "Hey Roxy. What brings you to the Murder

Room?" he asked. A term Rhodes had innocently coined, and which Wes had appropriated with relish.

Roxy laughed. "Don't you get started too. One loony per team is quite enough, thank you."

"Then where does that leave me?" Rhodes asked unexpectedly. He was leaning back against the white board, grinning.

Roxy peered at him, as surprised by his joking as Wes was.

"Behave," Roxy admonished. "I'm not in your league when it comes to crazy, and I come bearing information."

Rhodes practically quivered in anticipation.

"Although not of the good kind, I'm sorry to say," she continued. "Forensics has precisely zip connecting any of your crime scenes."

Fountain let out a deep sigh. "So, unless Gia comes up with a sex-club connection, I guess that's that then," he conceded.

"A sex-club connection?" Roxy mouthed at Wes, who just shook his head, a lopsided grin on his lips. She'd learn to just roll with Fountain's punches, the way the rest of the team was learning to.

The afternoon sun slanted rays of sunshine through the narrow windows as the team gathered around the conference room table. Wes cast one last look at them before placing the call to Detective Tolliver. Page had made him lead on the case, so the call was his to make. Putting the call on speaker so everyone could chime in if they felt the need to, he waited patiently for the man to pick up the phone at his end.

"So, tell me you have something for me," Tolliver said without preamble.

"I'm sorry, no." Wes told him. "Except for the similarities in location, we didn't find anything else that tied any of the victims together."

"Damn it," the Detective swore softly. "I was hoping we'd just missed something."

Across the table, Fountain's gaze sharpened, keying in on something Wes couldn't even begin to guess at, but he could practically hear the man's brain racing.

"Something you wanted to add, Rhodes?" he asked. He was beginning to recognize when something was going on in his partner's mind. A sharpening of focus, a slight shift in body language, an intensity that spilled over into the air around them.

"Um, yes. No. I just—" He shook his head impatiently, frustrated with himself, another sign Wes had learned meant the man's mind was working faster than his mouth could deal with. Taking a calming breath, he started over. "Detective Tolliver, was Mrs. Park missing anything?"

Around the table, the rest of the team members stirred, glancing at each other before looking back at the phone.

"Not that we know of. Her credit cards were still in her wallet along with"—they could hear pages rustling—"forty-two dollars, and her laptop and cell phone are accounted for. The only thing we couldn't find was her car key. One of those fob things. You know the ones that start the car without you putting the key in anything? We're checking around to see if maybe she set it down someplace and was heading back to get it. Which, I need to follow up on," he added mostly to himself. "But other than her key, she wasn't missing anything."

"Detective, we'll call you right back," Rhodes said urgently and before Tolliver could say anything else, Fountain reached out and ended the call.

"What?" Wes asked.

"We need to go back over our victims' personal effects, because Jaquille Shonte? He was also missing a key."

"A car key?" Talafiero asked. "I don't remember that."

"No, it was a safe key."

"And you know this why?"

"Because, in his interview, the man's partner specifically asked if it had been found. They'd just had a new safe installed at their studio, they design jewelry, and Shonte had the only copy."

"Why keys?" Talafiero asked a little while later. "I don't get it. Who takes keys for trophies?"

"A cagophilist," Fountain answered.

"A what?"

"A person who collects keys."

"And that's a thing?"

Fountain shrugged. "Why not? There are people who are entredentolignumologist's."

"Entre—*what?*"

"People who collect toothpick boxes."

"I don't even want to know why you'd know that."

"So, we're agreed?" Wes interrupted, before Rhodes could get started on the weird things people collected. Another thing he'd learned about the man: he knew a terrifying array of really bizarre facts.

Leaning back in his chair, Romano nodded. "Don't see how they *can't* be connected."

"Alleys, parking lots, and keys." Gia agreed. "Weird ass thing to collect though," she added under her breath.

"Better than kidneys," Rhodes said cheerfully.

Reaching for the phone, Wes stifled a laugh as he thought, *And I bet you know the name for that kind of collector too.*

"Detective Tolliver? We've found a link." Wes told him. "Every one of your victims was missing a key."

There was a long pause, then an audible sigh.

"A key. So, what you're telling me is that we have a serial killer loose in west L.A. with a key fetish."

"That's what it looks like, yes," Wes agreed.

"Start packing your bags then," Tolliver told them. "I'll be sending in a formal request for your assistance as soon as we hang up."

FOURTEEN

OBSERVATIONS

He had laid his trail meticulously. Adding new victims one by one. Surprisingly, it had been the idiots in West Hollywood who'd finally realized they had a serial killer, though it had been so much fun watching their bumbling antics until they'd caught on. He hadn't minded the wait at all. And now, here they were, his prize, the FBI in all their shiny glory, and best of all, the shrink was one of them. How unexpected and how utterly delicious, he thought, watching his local news anchor gushing over that tidbit as she stood in front of the West Hollywood precinct with all the rest of the paparazzi, hoping for a glimpse of the man in question.

He wondered how long it would take before the cops over in Beverly Hills realized they had a serial killer too. But the Santa Monica PD were being woefully slow; he'd have to liven things up a bit there to clue them in. At the rate they were going, those clods were never going to catch on. As for the LAPD, they'd catch on eventually. Or not.

It was a good thing the sun was shining today. He had a lot of planning to do. He intended to welcome the team from the FBI in a most spectacular way. He just hoped they were paying attention. He snorted. Well, if they weren't, they soon would be.

---

8 a.m.

"Special Agent Page? I'm Detective Tolliver. Thank you for coming."

Avery Tolliver was a medium tall, balding, middle-aged man whose face had seen a few punches. His nose was a little crooked, and several small white scars were peppered around his left eye, one through his eyebrow, the rest under it. His handshake was firm when he shook Page's hand, although he couldn't quite hide the very real worry in his steel-gray eyes, for which Page couldn't blame him. No one wanted a serial killer on their hands.

Behind Tolliver, heads turned as the officers of the West Hollywood station caught sight of the Special Investigations team, lips curling in disdain. Like they really *needed* the damn Feds interfering.

Then one of the officers leaned over, nudged his partner, and said, "Hey, look who the cat dragged in," loudly enough for Page to hear.

Giving the man an icy glare, he held the man's gaze for a

heartbeat before turning back to Tolliver and saying, "We're glad to help." Then gesturing at the men and women gathered behind him he added, "I'm sure you know Special Agents Romano and Talafiero from their time with the L.A. bureau office, and I believe you also know Special Agent Smith from a previous case as well?"

Tolliver nodded.

"And this is Special Agent Greene, our forensics specialist, and Dr. Rhodes, our expert on patterns."

"And movie stars," someone said loudly.

Detective Tolliver spun around, "*De Grassi!*" he bellowed warningly, but the man in question wasn't paying any attention to Tolliver; he was watching Rhodes instead.

"Um, no, not really," Rhodes said, shaking his head, as if the snide comment had been a question. "I don't watch many movies, actually."

For a second, the room went completely still as the officers stared at Rhodes in disbelief, then the phones which had gone silent at their arrival started ringing wildly again.

Oh good grief, thought Talafiero could he *be* any more naive?

Roxy Greene bit her lip to keep from laughing, while Romano and Page exchanged a look.

Wes laid a hand on his partner's shoulder.

"What?" asked Rhodes, confused by the whole thing, but Wes just shook his head.

"Nothing," he said quietly.

Page turned to Tolliver and asked, "If someone could show us where to set up our things, we'd like to brief your people on what we know so far."

"Uh, yeah," Tolliver answered, wondering if Rhodes could be any blonder. "The conference room's right over there, and I'll talk to De Grassi about bothering Rhodes," he added, so only Page could hear him.

"I'm more concerned about the media than any of your men." Page said bluntly. "How long do you figure it'll take before someone tells them he's here?"

"With that lot"—Tolliver said jerking his head toward the bullpen—"they probably know already."

9 a.m.

"So, where do you want to begin?" Tolliver asked, stepping aside as Romano and Wes lifted the last of the boxes they'd brought with them onto the conference room table, removed their lids, and started pulling out the stacks of papers that were in them.

Page considered the question as he looked around the room, noting with pride the seamless way the team was working together, as if they'd been together for years, not the few paltry weeks they had been. Wes and Romano had taken on the heavy lifting, while Rhodes was marking the crime scene locations on a map. At the back of the room, Talafiero was sorting through crime scene pictures, pinning them to the white boards that lined the wall.

The only person missing was Greene, who Page could see through the tall glass windows that separated the conference room from the bullpen. She was talking to Tolliver's sergeant, Sully, and a uniformed officer, her head canted to the side as she listened intently to what the officer was telling her.

"The crime scene locations," Page said finally in answer, a slight frown crossing his face as he noticed Rhodes staring intently at the map he'd been working on. Then in a flurry of motion, he spun around, grabbed up his laptop case, snagged a chair, sat down, pulled out his laptop, and started typing furiously.

"Not much to see. They're either parking lots or alleys people park in," Tolliver told him.

But instead of answering Tolliver, Page asked, "Rhodes? You have something?"

"Yeah, I do," he answered almost apologetically, swiveling the chair around as he looked up. "We were so focused on finding a connection between the homicides here in West Hollywood, we overlooked something. Inez Park was killed in a parking lot that both West Hollywood and Beverly Hills PD respond to. On April First."

"April Fool's Day," Wes said, immediately understanding where his partner was going.

"I don't get it," Tolliver said.

"April Fool's Day is a day people traditionally play tricks on each other," Fountain said, taking the man literally.

"Yeah, I know what it is." Tolliver said dryly.

"No. It's a day you *get fooled*."

Tolliver shrugged. "Okay. So how did he fool us?"

"He kept our eyes on West Hollywood. He knew squad cars would respond from both cities, but he also knew Beverly Hills wasn't going to fight you for jurisdiction in a homicide."

"So, the joke was on us. We never looked for recent homicides in Beverly Hills," Wes finished for him.

"And?" Page asked.

"And they've had three since March, if you include Inez Park." Fountain told him.

"Why didn't anyone know this?" Gia asked.

"Because we don't share information," Tolliver muttered. "So, the joke's on all of us."

Which is when Roxy stuck her head in through the open conference room doorway and said, "Page? I think you need to hear this."

"Hear what?"

"This is Officer Cranston," she answered, as Cranston followed her into the conference room, and Sully closed the door behind them. "Go ahead. Repeat what you told me."

Licking her lips nervously, Cranston glanced around the room before looking back at Page and saying, "Sir, my husband's a uniform with Santa Monica PD. And, well, we talk shop. You know how you do?"

Page made a murmuring assent.

"So, I didn't make the connection until after what you told us out there at the briefing."

"What connection?" Tolliver interrupted eyes fixed intently on her face.

"They had a homicide the end of March, sir, and then there was another one the beginning of April. I remembered thinking at the time how weird that was, because they don't get many and two so close together, well, they just stuck in my mind, because of the ones we'd had here too. Then Danny, my husband? Well, he was the responding officer to a third homicide a few weeks later, and after the uh, Special Agent finished telling us about how we might have a serial killer here, well, I thought there might be a connection, especially since they haven't been able to solve any of their murders either. So, I asked Danny to check if any of their victims were missing anything."

"And let me guess, they were all missing keys," Page finished for her. She nodded.

"Damn it," Tolliver cursed angrily.

"Thank you, Officer Cranston," Page said softly. "Tolliver, we'll need copies on everything Beverly Hills and Santa Monica have on their victims and the crime scenes."

"Well, that might take a little while." Tolliver answered. "As we've just proved, cooperation isn't our strong suit."

"I'll take care of that. Not cooperating with a federal investigation into a possible serial killer operating in their jurisdic-

tions? That isn't going to look good on the evening news."
Greene told him, reaching for her phone and walking out of the
conference room.

"Now there's a woman I wouldn't want to tangle with,"
Tolliver said in admiration. "I'm thinking you'll have copies of
their files in no time."

"That's what I'm counting on," Page told him. "All right,
Wes, I want you and Rhodes to start going through whatever
they send. Romano, Talafiero, head on over to the crime scenes
in Santa Monica. Detective, I want to see the crime scenes here
in West Hollywood before Greene and I go over to Beverly
Hills."

"Hope you brought your reading glasses," Wes teased as a
uniformed officer brought in the first stack of papers from
Santa Monica a short time later.

Tearing his gaze away from the pile he already had from
Beverly Hills, Rhodes frowned. "I don't wear glasses," he said,
sounding slightly offended.

"Not yet," Wes agreed, hiding a smile. "But by the time we're
done reading all these, we both might need them."

"That's not how it works," Rhodes protested, and then his
eyes widened slightly as he realized what Wes had been doing.
Lightening the moment before the grim set in.

Then very blandly, and much to Wes' surprise, he said,

"Well, I want ones with rhinestones. And they need to be huge, so I don't miss anything."

Laughing to himself, Wes made a mental note to try and find a pair just like that. Knowing Fountain, he'd probably wear them too.

FIFTEEN

OBSERVATIONS CONTINUED

THE END OF APRIL

He was enjoying himself immensely, watching the Special Investigations team work his case. He'd never heard of it before. Hadn't even known it existed, until he'd done a little Google search after his local news anchor mentioned it. And how flattering was that? Not only was the shrink here, but the newly formed unit was cutting its teeth on him. The best of the best. It was so . . . gratifying. He wondered what they thought so far of his little game. Wondered if they even knew they were playing, yet. He smiled, white teeth shining in the sun. He'd give them a day or two to finish catching up, but after that, all bets were off.

*** Noon***

"So, what have you got from Beverly Hills and Santa Monica?"

Page asked, striding into the conference room, followed closely by Romano, Greene, Talafiero, and Tolliver.

"Nothing that makes any sense," Rhodes murmured, glancing up briefly from the paper he was reading.

Tolliver rolled his eyes, and Wes could practically hear him thinking, "Great, the *airhead* was also their analyst?"

Romano stared at Rhodes closely. "Nothing?" he queried in disbelief.

Rhodes shrugged, pinched the top of his nose, then rubbed his eyes before saying, "What we have are six murders that are so clinically detached and sterile it's like the perpetrator was bored or something."

"Bored?" Page echoed, clearly disturbed at Rhodes terminology.

Rhodes nodded. "I don't know how else to describe it, Page. Each victim was dispatched quickly. Two were hit once with a blunt object, two were shot up close, and two were stabbed. The wounds were precise, ensuring a quick kill. Emotion just wasn't a part of the equation, and there's was no sexual component either."

"There also isn't any apparent motive," Wes picked up. "Like the kills here in West Hollywood, nothing was taken from any of the scenes. Money, phones, laptops, everything they had with them was accounted for. The sole exception being they were each missing a key."

"Which pretty much ensures the murders are tied in together," Romano said, placing bags of food on the end of the table. "Lunch," he said, looking across at Wes and Fountain.

While Tolliver asked, "House keys, or what?"

"House, car, office, gym locker." Wes shrugged.

"So, whatever they had on them, then?"

Rhodes nodded. "Like the others, yes."

"What about a geographical profile?" Page asked.

"The only thing that's coming to mind is state route two. All three towns have access off of it," Fountain said, absent mindedly waving his hand in the general direction of the map behind him, his eyes focused on the bag of food and the sandwiches Romano was pulling out of it.

"State route two?" Roxy asked, pulling soft drinks out of a second bag.

"It's basically Santa Monica Boulevard until it runs into the one-oh-one. Then it squiggles around L.A. before going out to Angeles National Forest," Romano told her.

"Victimology?" Page asked, taking a soda and a brown-paper-wrapped sub marked "pastrami."

"Nothing there, either," Wes told him. "Two Caucasian, two African American, one Mexican, and one Puerto Rican."

"So, an equal-opportunity killer," Talafiero said, sighing.

Wes nodded. "Pretty much. If anything, this is starting to look like he's picking his victims at random."

"Wonderful," Tolliver muttered.

"Thoughts?" Page asked.

Rhodes took a sub from Romano marked, "roast beef" with a murmured, "Thank you."

"The crimes are too polished, too . . .practiced," Wes said slowly, accepting a sub marked "turkey w. cranberry mayo." "He had to have started somewhere else. There's no learning curve here. There's nothing messy or sloppy about these kills. He knew what he was doing already."

"Agreed, and I'm guessing he started here in West Hollywood," Page said, reaching into a third sack and pulling out bags of potato chips, pretzels, and apple slices, which he tossed into the center of the table within easy reach of everybody. "We need to go back and figure out when he started."

"We've got a few unsolveds from last year, but they're pretty different from these." Tolliver said, gesturing at the crime scene photographs on the wall with one hand, while taking a ham and cheese with the other.

"Anything you can give us from, let's say, the last six months would be a good place to start."

"I'll get someone right on it."

"Um, no need," Rhodes mumbled, fingers flying over the keys of his laptop. "Apparently, there were three. A strangling, an entire family wiped out, and a man stabbed in an alley."

Tolliver's eyes narrowed, his lips thinning as he looked across at Rhodes.

"If we could get those files then," Page said, the twitch of a smile crossing his own lips. "And Rhodes, stop hacking into computer systems, please."

"Um, oh. Sorry," Rhodes said, not sounding the least bit sorry to Wes's ears as he closed the lid on his laptop and opened his sub instead.

"Which just leaves contacting Santa Monica and Beverly Hills after lunch to see if they have any unsolveds from last year that might fit our parameters. The old-fashioned way," Page added, with a pointed look at Rhodes. "By calling."

** 4 p.m. **

When Rhodes's phone rang, he answered it without checking the read out, assuming it was Greene calling from somewhere else, since she was the only team member not in the room at the moment. "You're on speaker, Greene. What's up?"

"I suppose it would help if I *were* Greene," came the familiar husky voice recognizable to millions around the world.

Grinning widely, Wes called out, "Hi, Molly," and before Rhodes could snatch up his phone to take her off speaker, her laugh rang out across the room. "That *has* to be Wes!"

Talafiero burst out laughing, even as Page and Romano exchanged uncharacteristic grins.

"*Molly!*" Rhodes exclaimed, turning his back on the team for a little privacy.

"Serves you right," she teased. "So where are you, gorgeous?"

"L.A.," Rhodes said still flustered.

"You're kidding!"

"Um, no?"

"Where?" she demanded.

"West Hollywood?"

"Good! Then you can meet me for dinner!"

How could he—and then his mind cleared. "You're here?" he exclaimed. For some reason, he'd thought she was still in Hawaii.

"Yes," she laughed. "So, can you meet me?"

He cast a dubious eye on Page, thinking no way in hell he'd agree. "Um."

"Wait! Bring the team too."

"What?"

"The team . . . bring the team, my treat, eight o'clock at Torelli's." And she hung up before he could answer her. For a minute he just stared at the phone.

"Trouble in paradise?" Wes teased.

Huh? "Uh, no. I just didn't know she was also in L.A."

"And?" Wes prodded.

"She invited all of us to dinner."

Romano leaned back, grinning. "Did she now? Where and when?"

"Um, eight o'clock at Torelli's?"

"Torelli's?" Romano exclaimed.

"I take it that's a good thing?" Roxy asked.

"Trust me," Romano agreed grinning broadly. "Especially if she's paying. What do you say, Page?"

"I say that only gives us three hours to finish reading through these old case files and still have time to go get cleaned up before we meet her there." Page said unexpectedly. "No one in their right minds gives up a chance to eat at Torelli's."

Three hours later, as the day was fading away, turning the sky outside the long narrow windows in the conference room from blue to orange to rose, a last tiny flare of brilliant yellows and reds painted the sky as the sun sank below the building opposite them.

Leaning back in his chair, Wes stretched his arms over his head, feeling his back crack, before slumping down again. He was beyond tired. Facts and figures swam in his head.

Cold cups of coffee stood forgotten in front of each member of the team, mute testimony to the intensity to which they'd applied themselves in trying to find out everything they could about the killer.

"All right, so I think it's safe to say that those three unsolveds here in West Hollywood last year were his." Wes said, gesturing at the files they'd pulled out from the teetering stacks around them. "Part of his learning curve, if you will, to see what excited him."

They'd all been messy. The strangling, the stabbing, and the family of four shot at the dinner table. Although, he wasn't sure about that one—it had a different feel to it.

"And that neither Santa Monica nor Beverly Hills have anything that even remotely resembles them."

Page looked around the table. "Agreed. Anything else?" When no one answered, he stood up briskly and said, "Then I think we're done here for now. Let's head over to the hotel and freshen up before dinner."

God yes, Wes thought. He could use a shower.

"Then we can get a good night's sleep and start over again in the morning. I think we need to take another look at locations and timelines. Someone, somewhere saw something."

"Sounds good to me," Romano agreed.

One by one the team gathered up their things and headed for the door. Wes paused in the act of turning out the lights when he realized Rhodes was still working. "Hey, Rhodes, we're leaving!"

"I'll be along in a little bit. There's something I want to check out," Fountain mumbled, hunched over his laptop, fingers flying over the keys.

Wes shook his head. "Then you're going to miss dinner with your own girlfriend." And judging by the startled look on the man's face, Wes knew he'd forgotten about it. He had to fight to hide a grin as the man scrambled to his feet in a flurry of arms and legs, shoving his laptop into its case.

"Ready," he said a heartbeat later, dragging a hand through his hair and snagging his jacket from the back of the chair. "How do I look?" he asked anxiously.

"Like something the cat dragged in. But no need to worry,"

Wes added cheerfully at Rhodes horrified look. "You've got plenty of time to shower and change before we meet up with Molly."

"What are we supposed to wear?" Rhodes asked worriedly as they walked through the nearly empty bullpen.

"Clothes, Rhodes. Clothes."

"Funny," Rhodes shot back.

"Try a jacket and tie. Something that goes together would be nice," he added, thinking about the man's penchant for being slightly off kilter when it came to dressing. "Although," he added with a slight grin, "apparently it doesn't matter what you wear. Molly loves you anyway."

** 8 p.m. **

The valets didn't even try to park the black SUV; they simply directed the behemoth into the shadows where it couldn't be seen from the street. Torelli's was known to be discreet in everything.

"Ah, ladies, gentlemen," the maître d' greeted them. "This way, if you please," he said without even inquiring as to who they might be. Romano smiled at Wes; this was definitely his kind of place. "And will you be drinking this evening?" the maître d' added after seating them at a secluded round table at the back of the restaurant.

"Yes, we'll be drinking," Romano assured him.

"Excellent," the maître d' said, smiling. "Henri will take your orders."

"Where's Rhodes?" Talafiero asked, sipping gratefully on a bourbon a short time later.

"Saying a private hello to Molly, I imagine," Page said, eyes on the menu. "And although I know I don't have to, may I remind you all to please behave, because—in case you haven't noticed—these menus have no prices on them, which means everything on them is well above your pay grades, and that Ms. Whittier is very kindly paying for dinner this evening."

"Speaking of the devil," Romano added softly.

"Special Agent in Charge Page!" Molly exclaimed, grinning. "Congratulations on your promotion!"

"You're going to do that every time you see me, aren't you?" Page said, smiling.

"Yes, *Thomas*, I am," she said wickedly. "And you must be Nico Romano," she added winking at Page before turning toward Romano.

"Oh, I like you already!" Romano exclaimed.

"Of course you do," she replied saucily. Romano laughed.

"And *you* are quite definitely Wes," she said fanning herself. "Is it getting hot in here, ladies, or is it just me?" she asked, shooting a sly grin at Gia and Roxy.

"Molly!" Rhodes exclaimed as Wes burst out laughing.

"I *definitely* like your lady, Rhodes!"

"Molly, I'm Gia," Talafiero said, grinning. "And this is Roxy, and Wes's girlfriend is going to be *so* mad she missed out on meeting you," she added.

"Oh, we can remedy that!" Molly said, grinning conspiratorially. "How about a lady's night out next time we're all in D.C.?"

"You're on!" Talafiero said.

"Why is it," Romano interrupted, "that I wish I were going to be a fly on the wall for that?"

"I have *no* idea at all," Molly said innocently, slipping her hand into Rhodes's under the table and giving it a gentle squeeze. "And why didn't I know you had a girlfriend, Wes? Rhodes, you are the worst gossip!" Molly scolded.

"I didn't know," he protested.

"Don't feel bad," Wes told him. "I didn't know I had a girlfriend either."

"Don't be ridiculous. Your next-door neighbor, Harriet? The one who's been cooking you dinner every evening," Roxy said, grinning.

"Harry," Wes corrected. "She goes by Harry. And we're not dating." Were they? "She's my neighbor, and I only just met her a few weeks ago!"

"Keep telling yourself that," Roxy said, grinning at him. "She's cooking for you, taking you furniture shopping. Probably picking up your dry cleaning, so, yeah, that pretty much makes her your girlfriend, I'm thinking."

. . .

"Well, at least they don't drool on each other," Talafiero said later that night on the drive back to the hotel. Rhodes and Molly had disappeared together into the back of a discreet black Lincoln once dinner was over.

"Drool?" Wes asked, biting back a snort.

"If I were dating Molly Whittier, trust me, I'd be drooling," Romano said, laughing.

"So, what do you think?" Gia asked Page curiously.

Page glanced up at her in the rearview mirror. "Think about what?"

Romano looked sideways at Page. "About Molly and Rhodes is what!" he said exasperatedly.

"They make a nice couple."

"They make a *nice couple?*"

Page shrugged. "They look like two young people who are in love."

The two young people in question were wrapped around each other in the back of the town car. Lips swollen from kisses, fingers tangled in each other's hair.

"Missed you," Fountain whispered.

"Just a few more weeks," Molly promised, "then I'll be home for at least a month."

He hated to ask, but the words crept out before he could stop them. "Home with me, or home with your mom?"

"With you," she promised. "Except for a day or two here and

there, because, well, she's my mom, and you won't even notice. You'll be busy working on some case."

"I always notice when I'm not with you," he said, cupping her face. And his words took her breath away, as did the kiss that followed them.

Tongues tangled and teeth clashed, and they giggled, resting their foreheads together.

"I could fall in love with your house," she told him.

"It comes with the guy who owns it."

"I could fall in love with him too," she whispered.

"Good," he answered, "because he's already in love with you."

"Fountain?" She leaned back and looked into his eyes.

"Love you, Molly," he told her, and she couldn't help the smile that lit up her face.

"Love you too," she whispered and this time when his lips caught hers, she could taste forever on them.

"I'm sorry for interrupting, Miss Whittier, but do you want me to keep driving?" Molly's driver, Stan, asked a few minutes later. "Miss O'Brien's car is in the driveway," he added by way of explanation.

Tearing away from Fountain's kiss, Molly looked up, meeting Stan's eyes in the rearview mirror. Ricki was here? Why now, damn it? She was half tempted to tell him to keep on going, but knowing Ricki she'd just keep on waiting.

"No, it's fine, Stan." And then to Fountain she said, "I'm sorry."

"Do you want me to stay in the car while you talk to her?" Fountain asked, knowing how much Molly's manager disliked him.

"No," Molly told him firmly. "She can just get over it. We're together. End of story." Together and in love, she thought giddly to herself. Ricki was going to have a fit.

"Molly, where have you been?" Ricki said sharply, pouncing on her before she'd barely gotten out of the car. "I've got these scripts for you to look over and—oh. I didn't know *he* was here." Her lip curled as Fountain got out of the car behind Molly.

"Well, as you can see, *he* is. So, good night, Ricki. We'll talk about the scripts tomorrow."

"Fine," Ricki snarled. "Not that you'll be alone," she added, smugly. "Michael's here."

"Of course he is, Ricki. He lives here, just like Jonathon," Molly answered over her shoulder as she opened the front door and tugged Fountain through it.

As they stepped into the house, Fountain caught a glimpse of someone jogging past—a weird time to be out running he thought, but then Molly kissed him, and he forgot everything except for the feel of her lips against his.

"She really doesn't like me," Fountain sighed as the door closed.

"Good thing her opinion doesn't count then," Molly told

him, taking a kiss. "Come on. Let's go say hi to Michael, then maybe we can steal a few hours together, unless you can stay the night?"

Pulling her into his arms, Fountain touched their foreheads together. "I wish, but if something happens, I need to be with the team."

"Thought that was your voice I heard, Fountain," Michael said, peering down the hallway. "Don't let me intrude—I was just getting a snack. But it's good to see you." He tilted his head a bit. "Did I know you were coming? Did you know you were coming?"

"No, and no," Fountain answered, laughing, as they joined Michael in the living room.

"Good. I haven't been myself lately, to be honest, and I think I've been forgetting too many things. Staff meetings, tests, getting my oil changed."

"That's not unusual after something traumatic happens, but it does get better," he told his friend.

"Everything's just been such a mess. I mean, not only did someone murder Anna, but now they can't find her office key anyplace, so they're having to replace all the locks. Like someone is going to steal something from us," he scoffed. "We're mathematicians, for god's sake."

And Fountain went still at Michael's words.

"Fount, what is it?" Molly asked.

"I have to get back to the station. There's something I have to check," he answered, getting up. "God, Moll, I'm so sorry."

"Was it something I said?" Michael asked.

"Yes. And I think it's important."

"Stan won't have gone far, I'll call him back—" Molly started.

"No, I'll just get an Uber. It's late and—"

"He's two minutes out."

"Moll, he doesn't have to—"

"No, he doesn't. But this way I can spend a little more time with you." And Fountain felt his heart go bump.

SIXTEEN

THE DA VINCI THING

Hmmmm. Well, that was interesting, he thought, watching as the taillights on Molly Whittier's car disappeared into the morning traffic. He wondered if Mr. FBI Agent knew his girlfriend had been out having breakfast with that obnoxious git Martin Riley today. True, her red-headed manager had been with them, but still. Fodder for the grist mill.

No doubt there would be some ridiculous headline in one of the tabloids tomorrow screaming about their breakup. Which he doubted. Not with the way Whittier and Rhodes had been kissing last night as he'd jogged by her house.

And certainly not with Mr. Martin Riley. Now there was a prize pompous ass. He'd just had to sit outside today and not at just any table. Nooooo. It had to be the right one, where he could be seen by everyone going past.

And the guy was rude, too. He was their waiter, not the asshats servant. But the Fed's girlfriend had been nice. Hadn't treated him like a "thing." The red-headed chick—he thought she was also Riley's manager from the way she was talking, how convenient to be repping both of them—had been somewhere in between. Expecting him to hover, so he'd be nearby if they needed him, while still being discreet.

He could do discreet, all right. It's how you overheard the best things. One of the perks of waitering, so he hadn't minded that part one bit. Especially when their talk had turned away from some movie the Fed's girlfriend didn't seem to be too interested in being in, and on to more exciting topics. Like, the FBIs investigation into the serial killer in their midst.

Ha! If they'd only known the truth of just how close they'd been to him. Riley probably would have fainted. He snickered at the thought of that.

Still, it had been worth putting up with him to learn the shrink had tumbled onto one part of the game he'd laid out for them—the missing keys that tied all the recent murders in West Hollywood, Beverly Hills and Santa Monica together. The police chiefs in Beverly Hills and Santa Monica must have had a cow when they realized they hadn't even noticed they had a serial killer preying on their residents. And now the shrink had tied in Dr. Stone, too. That must have caused an uproar! Give the Fed two points! But that guy, Riley? He'd shoot him in a heartbeat if the opportunity ever arose, especially after the lousy tip he left him.

"I wonder when 'the boyfriend' is going to crawl into work

today?" Romano was saying, a grin on his face, as he and Talafiero walked into the conference room the next morning. He stopped dead two feet into the room and stared at the mayhem in front of him.

Folders were stacked in untidy piles all over the conference table, and Rhodes was writing frantically on one of the white boards.

"Uh, Rhodes, what the hell's going on?"

Startled, Rhodes whipped around to face them. "God, you scared me."

"Apparently," Wes agreed, coming into the room behind them, getting a look at the mayhem for himself. Then gesturing at the table, he asked, "What's all this about?"

"So, there's a murder you didn't know about, because I didn't tell you, because I didn't think it was related until last night when Molly's brother told me that Professor Stone was also missing a key, something I hadn't known, or I'd have told you," he said in one long, out-of-breath sentence.

Wes blinked.

"Okay. Let's break that down. Who is Professor Stone, and when did he get murdered?"

"She. Anna. I knew her. She was a professor at CalTech, and someone shot her in the parking garage on April fifth."

"CalTech," Gia said. "That's in Pasadena, Fount."

"Yes. I know it is."

"A little out of our kill zone, isn't it?"

"Is it?" he countered.

And very quietly Romano said, "Oh, shit."

"What makes you think the cases are connected?" Page asked.

"The missing key, for one. And, I um, might have dragged someone I know out of bed last night to run a comparison between the bullet that killed her and the other shootings that we know of."

"That has to be one hell of a connection," Romano said, admiringly. "No one jumps the line at ballistics."

"What were the results?" Page asked, having come in with Wes.

"The same gun killed all of them. There's something else too. Jacarta called me back a little while ago. You know that family that was murdered last year here in West Hollywood? They're also a match."

"But they don't fit our profile. They're—personal," Romano murmured.

"I think Professor Stone might have been personal too," Fountain said sadly.

"Which leads us back to this," Wes said, gesturing at the stacks of files again.

"Remember yesterday when I said the new murders in Santa Monica and Beverly Hills seemed clinical? Well, that's exactly what they were!" He waved a hand at the crime scene photos pinned to the white board behind him. "Just like the ones in West Hollywood, they were carried out systematically, one after the other, so even the blindest cop could figure out there was a serial killer at work there! The perpetrator *wanted* to be sure the police realized they were dealing with a serial killer, so they'd have no choice but to call us!"

"And it worked very nicely too," Romano said dryly.

"Why would he want us here?" Talafiero asked. "I mean, he could have gone undetected for who knows how long."

"Because, once he figured out what he did and didn't like, he got bored just randomly killing people, waiting for someone to notice him. So he decided to play a game, to see if anyone would notice him then. Look!"

Turning, Rhodes grabbed a pile of the newest crime scene photos and added them as a separate grouping beside the first ones in West Hollywood.

"*These* murders," he said pointing at them, "were committed in two different jurisdictions, but when you look at them side by side, you can see they share the *same pattern* as the original murders that brought us here. He's been committing overlapping cluster murders for months, but until I put them side by side, I didn't see it."

"And I'm still not seeing it," Romano said, just as Talafiero asked, "Cluster murders?"

"Groupings of murders that share an identical MO," Rhodes said impatiently. "The stabbings are one cluster. The shootings are another, the bludgeoning's are a third. So what at first glance appear to be random acts of violence are really carefully orchestrated murders.

"That's not all," Fountain plowed on. "If you count Mrs.

Park's murder for both West Hollywood and Beverly Hills, there's another cluster. Specifically, types of *locations* where they were murdered." And grabbing up a marker, he started writing on a white board.

Mrs. Inez and Donna Young hit over the head in grocery store parking lots.

Enrique Hernandez, Mary Fiennes, and Ronald Blythe, stabbed after leaving coffee shops.

Patrick Flaherty, Maria Lopez, and Patrick Howell, shot in alleys, going to or from their cars.

"And when you put them together," Wes said slowly, "you get clusters within clusters."

"How could we have missed them?" Tolliver asked, stunned.

"Because you weren't looking for them," Page answered.

"Wait, what about Jacquille Shonte?" Gia asked, frowning. "He fits into the 'how' cluster, but not the 'where' one, since he was hit over the head in an alley behind his business, not while he was out grocery shopping."

"So he's an anomaly," Romano grunted.

Rhodes nodded. "In more ways than one. That rebar he was hit with? It was part of a pile of construction debris, not something the killer brought with him."

"Which means his killing was spur of the moment," Wes said, thoughtfully. "A lot like Patrick Howell's and that family . . ."

"Which would make another cluster," Talafiero said softly.

"What happens if you add time of death?" Roxy asked, frowning.

"It gets worse," Rhodes said apologetically.

"Worse, how?"

"Like this." And cleaning off another space on the white board, Fountain wrote:

First thing in the morning—stab someone.

Early afternoon—bludgeon someone.

Early evening—shoot someone.

"So, basically breakfast, lunch, and dinner," Wes muttered.

"Murder by rote," Romano added, a slight frown on his face. "Except for your professor, who was shot first thing in the morning out in Pasadena."

"Which could mean there's another cluster out there somewhere," Page said quietly. Then gesturing at the cascading files, he added, "Was that what you were looking for?"

"Yes . . . No . . . Yes. I found the start of one in Century City. A man was hit across the back of the head with a golf club after doing some grocery shopping at a local mom-and-pop shop the afternoon of April third, and a woman was stabbed right after getting her morning coffee just last week on April twenty-first, also in Century City. There was also a stabbing not far from a coffee shop in Hollywood on April eleventh. But there's something else going on. Something I can't put my finger on."

"What makes you think that?" Romano asked intently.

Rhodes ran his fingers through his hair, tugging on it, gathering his thoughts. "Because these first ones," he said, gesturing at the original crime scene photographs, "they were just the breadcrumbs to get us here. The perpetrator could have cared less about them. And these"—he gestured at the second cluster —"it's like they were just a test to see if anyone was paying attention. To see if someone would notice he was playing a game yet. But any profiler would have found them sooner or later. So there's something else, something besides another cluster . . . something he doesn't think we're going to find, because he's sure he's smarter than we are."

"So, this game he's playing—what is it?" Page asked

"I don't know. All I do know is that we're playing it, too, and he's the only one who knows the rules."

For a second, it was very quiet as the team looked at one another.

"All right, someone somewhere saw something," Page said briskly. "Romano, Talafiero, take the coffee shops. Grill the baristas and anyone else who thinks they may have seen our perpetrator. Get them together with the police sketch artist in whatever jurisdiction you're in. We need his likeness out there.

"Greene, we're going back to the grocery stores. I want to see the surveillance tapes where Mrs. Park was killed and talk to the owners of the mom-and-pop shop. Wes, I want you and Rhodes to go back through everything we have. See if you can find what we're missing. Questions?"

"Um, more of a suggestion for Nico and Gia, really," Rhodes said. "You might want to go to the coffee shop here in West Hollywood first, where Mary Fiennes was stabbed with the knitting needle? Because knit groups tend to meet at the same time and place every week. Which means, they'd be there now."

"And you know this how?" Gia asked, a grin dancing on her lips.

"Because that's what my mom's knit group does."

"And here I thought you had a secret hobby," Gia said, laughing.

"No. Although Molly's promised to teach me," Rhodes said, smiling as if the thought made him happy.

Across the room Nico stared at him in disbelief, while Wes covered a snort of laughter with a cough, and Gia murmured, "Of course she did," with a little head shake and a grin of her own.

"So, what did you find out?" Page asked, once Romano and Talafiero had gotten cups of coffee and sat down. A box with a variety of pastries and fruits stood open on the table, the mom-and-pop shop having turned out to be a cross between a bakery, a fruit stand, and a deli. While Gia selected a donut twist, Romano grabbed a handful of grapes.

"That none of the parking lots at the coffee shops had surveillance cameras or windows overlooking them," Romano said, tossing a grape into his mouth. "Um, good," he added.

Licking sugar off her fingers, Gia picked up their narrative. "According to the baristas at the coffee shop in Beverly Hills, our perpetrator is a nondescript youngish male who likes to tap his fingernails on tables. Medium height, medium build, light brown hair," Gia told them. "He drives an older white midsize American-made car. But the barista who told us that wasn't sure as to the make or model, but he was positive he saw the guy getting into it.

"One of the knitters in West Hollywood distinctly remembers the tapping and how annoying Mrs. Fiennes found it. Apparently, she was counting stitches, and the tapping kept making her lose her place, so she packed up and left."

Nodding Romano glanced down at his notes before adding, "They all thought he was in his early twenties. He was wearing jeans and a Lakers hoodie, but other than that, their description was the same as the baristas."

"Why didn't we know this?" Tolliver asked, a flash of anger creeping into his voice. "I sent people out to get statements."

Gia nodded. "The baristas mentioned that. But apparently all your guys did was show them photos of the victims and asked if they remembered them."

To which Tolliver muttered some very choice words.

"In Beverly Hills, we found two witnesses who regularly go to the coffee shop where Ronald Blythe was killed. They both remembered a guy tapping his nails and how annoying it was, since they were trying to work," Romano continued. "One of the witnesses, who knew Blythe well enough to stop and chat with him when they were in there, said he was pretty sure Blythe had words with the guy. He was typing up a landscaping proposal, and the tapping was breaking his concentration. The witness said he heard Blythe politely ask the perpetrator to stop several times before becoming angry. The witness also said that the perpetrator seemed to think it was 'entertaining' when Blythe got mad, his word."

"The other witness said she heard someone else ask him to stop and when he didn't, they got up and moved tables, farther away from him," Greene went on, as Romano helped himself to a cheese Danish. "Other than that, same description, which was also confirmed by the baristas in Santa Monica. Medium build, brownish hair, tapped his fingers on the table just a little off beat from the music. One of them thought he got into it a little with Hernandez over something, but he wasn't sure it was the day Hernandez was killed. All of the witnesses are with sketch artists now, so we should have something in the next few hours."

"How'd it go with the video surveillance?" Wes asked.

"It was pretty much a bust," Roxy answered. "The mom-and-pop shop didn't have any, and there were sections of the parking lot where Mrs. Park was killed that weren't covered, so we're thinking that was something the perpetrator knew. Either by surveillance, or he might have worked there at one time."

"And while the owners of the corner store definitely recognized the picture of Donna Young, they both agreed she left the store with an older lady the night she was murdered. They said she often talked to other customers there, so it's possible our perpetrator struck up a conversation with her at some point while she was shopping and killed her once the other woman was gone."

"So, basically most of these people were simply in the wrong place at the wrong time," Tolliver said, frowning.

Which is when Rhodes phone rang.

Knowing who it most likely was, Page took a quick look at his watch and said, "Let's take a ten-minute break—consider everything we've just heard."

"You're welcome to use my office," Tolliver added, to which Rhodes mumbled a grateful, "Thank you," and hurried that way. Not answering the video call until he'd closed the door behind him.

"Hi," he said, just a little breathlessly.

"Hi, yourself," Molly answered, smiling. "Where are you?" she added, peering behind him.

"Um, Detective Tolliver's office."

"That explains the dead fish on the wall, then," she said, giggling. Which, of course, made Fountain look, and there was a very dead pike mounted on the wall behind him.

"I guess?"

"So, how's it going?" she asked, drawing his gaze back to her face.

"We have a description of the guy now, so it's going well I guess?"

"Is he creepy looking?"

"Um. Only if sort of ordinary is creepy."

"No, then," Molly said. "Creepy is a six-foot-one-inch, gym-muscled, dude with dark hair, blue eyes, and a cleft in his chin."

"Riley's bothering you again?" Rhodes asked, recognizing the description instantly.

"In his own way. At that meeting this morning, about the movie I don't want to make, he asked me if I was done, and I quote, 'playing around' with you yet."

And Fountain couldn't help a softly laughed, "God, I hope not."

Molly rolled her eyes. Then said, "Hang on a sec. I need to change needles."

"What are you knitting?" Rhodes asked, trying to peer down the phones screen, like that would help him see it somehow.

"A sock. For Michael. Although, you'd probably like the pattern too." She held it up, and he got an eyeful of dark blue with stripes unevenly placed on it."

"Um. Very nice?" he hazarded, because it looked like a bit of a mess to him, if he were being completely honest.

"What?" She glanced at the sock, then laughed, and pulled it back from the camera's eye. "Oops, had it too close to really see. So, what do you think?"

He blinked and stared really hard at it. Why did it look familiar?

"It's a Fibonacci sock pattern, which I thought was appropriate for the math professor."

A Fibonacci—"Molly, I have to go. You're brilliant! I'll tell you later." And then he was sprinting down the hallway back to the conference room.

"Fount, what is it?" Wes asked. The whole team startled by his sudden reappearance.

"The wrong place . . ." he mumbled, ignoring the question as he dug through the papers on the table. "The wrong place . . ." Then, grabbing up the one he wanted, he whipped around and said, "Not the wrong place, the wrong *date!*

"See? It's the wrong date!" he said excitedly. "It's not the eleventh it's the first!" Then turning to the white board, he started rearranging the order of the shootings.

"Rhodes, what the hell are you talking about?" Romano asked.

"The stabbing in Hollywood. I wrote it down as being on the eleventh, but it wasn't, it was on the first! I didn't check the written report—I used the coroner's report because it was stapled on top and look, the coroner's pen didn't work. See . . . he was scrubbing at the paper. That's why there are two marks on it! Brian Casey was killed on the *first!*"

"And this is important why?" Gia asked.

"Because our perpetrator is killing in a Fibonacci sequence. I just didn't see it before!"

"The Da Vinci thing?" Wes queried.

"Yes! It's part of the game he's playing! Look!"

And quickly Rhodes wrote the beginning of a Fibonacci sequence on the board:

1 1 2 3 5 8 13 21

"The same as the *dates* he killed most of his victims on," Page murmured.

"Exactly!" Rhodes enthused, adding names next to the dates.

April 1st—Inez Park and Brian Casey

April 2nd—Donna Young

April 3rd—Wei Chen

April 5th—Professor Stone

April 8th—Maria Lopez

April 13th—Patrick Flaherty

Viewed in a column it was chilling.

"There's more," Rhodes added. "We've got corresponding kills in March. Patrick Howell was killed on the eighth, Ronald Blythe was killed on the thirteenth, and Enrique Hernandez was killed on the twenty-first.

"He's overlapping his clusters," Wes murmured. "And since his earlier kills don't follow the pattern, that means he started playing his game in March."

"I don't get it. Why didn't he continue this Fibonacci thing? Why stop both months on the twenty-first?" Tolliver asked.

"Because the next number would be thirty-four, and there isn't a thirty-fourth in any of our months," Fountain answered, squinting at the white board myopically.

"Who would know that? About the Fibonacci thing?"

"Someone studying math."

"So, the perpetrator's what, a college student?"

Rhodes nodded. "Possibly. Or a math teacher, maybe?"

"So, that means"—Tolliver stopped for a moment, studying the white board—"that means. Shit. Tomorrow's May first. So if he continues his pattern, we can expect another murder."

"No," Rhodes said softly. "It means if he keeps to his pattern he'll kill twice tomorrow. The Fibonacci sequence begins with 1, 1."

For a minute, the room went silent.

"Ah, hell," Romano breathed softly.

"Earlier, you said this was only part of his game," Page said, sharply, focused on Rhodes. "What's the rest of it?"

Rhodes shook his head. "I don't know," he said quietly. "But it's almost as if his early kills were just for his own entertainment. Then something changed. Something happened. Something caught his interest."

"When was this?" Romano asked.

"I think it must have been the end of February, because his first kills, the *very* earliest ones, he was just playing . . . *learning* to kill. They were all one-off murders with no rhyme or reason or pattern. A testing of the waters so to speak. Like he was taunting the police, saying, hey guys, look over here, you've got a serial killer."

"Or waiting to see if they could put two and two together," Page said grimly.

"Trying to catch our attention," Tolliver said sourly.

"So, what happened at the end of February?" Page asked. "What was his trigger? What made him invent his game."

"It had to have been a major event," Greene said. "Something we shouldn't be missing."

Tolliver looked around at them in disbelief. "You're kidding, right?" Six pairs of eyes stared at him. "This is *Hollywood* . . . the Academy Awards happened!"

"Oh," Rhodes said softly. "So I was the catalyst."

"Whoa, you don't know that!" Roxy said quickly.

But Romano nodded. "That seems about right. Not you specifically, Fount, but what you represent. He'd been playing games for months without anyone noticing, and he was feeling pretty smart. Then he sees you on TV, and bingo! He decides what he really needs is a challenge. What he needs is the FBI to play his game with him."

For a moment, it was quiet.

"I think you're right. But that still doesn't tell me what the game *is*. All we know now is who's playing."

"And *when* he's playing," Page added darkly, then, looking around, he added, "I think we're ready to call a press conference. Talafiero, I want you at the podium, Detective Tolliver, if we could get copies of the police sketches to hand out to the press?"

"Not a problem. When do you want to do this? I think all the major news outlets are outside already. I'm not sure they've ever left since you got here."

"Thirty minutes should give them enough time to notify their stations and for us to brief your people first. Roxy, get Santa Monica and Beverly Hills hooked into the briefing and make sure they have copies of the artist sketches too."

Page looked out at the faces of the people in front of him. Their resentment at the presence of the FBI was palpable, made even more so because they weren't "their" FBI; they were outsiders horning in on their turf.

He waited for the nod from Greene, signaling the two other jurisdictions were watching on video feed, and started. "We have reason to believe that the man in the sketches you've been handed is responsible for a series of murders stretching along a corridor from Santa Monica to Pasadena. He is a white male, between the ages of twenty and thirty, with medium brown hair, and either brown or hazel eyes," Page stated.

"He's of average height and build with no outstanding characteristics. He's been seen getting into an older white American compact car, possibly a Chevrolet or Buick.

"It's possible he's a student at one of the local universities, studying mathematics. He'll also be a loner with few, if any, social skills," he added, as Rhodes began tapping on a desk, drawing questioning looks from the officers closest to him.

"He makes people feel uneasy whenever he's around. He enjoys annoying people. Getting a rise out of them. Like that," Page said, as the officers in the room with them began to get restless, glancing from Page to Rhodes and then back again. "Exactly like that," he told them.

"We know it's how he picked out several of his victims who were either working at or visiting with friends at local coffee shops. He began tapping his fingers then waited to see who asked him to stop, and when he wouldn't, and they left, he followed them outside and stabbed them."

"We also know he's bludgeoned several people in grocery store parking lots and that he's not afraid to use a gun either."

"Excuse me, sir, how do you know it's all the same person? With the different MOs, it sounds more like three different people." A uniform at the front of the room asked.

"Because of the trophies he's taken," Page answered. "In each case, the victim was missing a key—a fact we'd like to keep to ourselves for the moment."

"So, we're looking for an annoying generic-looking white guy who's a nerd and has a key fetish?" Di Grassi asked, grinning.

"We're looking for a serial killer," Page corrected him coldly.

"I'm Special Agent Gia Talafiero with the Special Investigations Unit of the FBI," Gia said, looking out at the mob of reporters clustered around the station's steps. "I have a brief statement to make about an ongoing investigation into multiple homicides stretching from Santa Monica to Pasadena, after which I'll take your questions."

"Is it true that Dr. Rhodes is part of the team the FBI sent here?" someone shouted when she was through with her official statement.

"Is he a profiler?"

"Does he carry a gun?"

"Has he ever killed anyone?"

"Well, that went well," Wes said, when the press conference was over, shaking his head in disbelief. "I don't think a single reporter asked a question about the serial killer . . ."

SEVENTEEN

THE GOLDEN RULE

How dare they! Who did they think they were, warning people to stay off the streets tomorrow? He raged, slamming his fists down on the table. Now look at what they'd made him do! The peas were in the mashed potatoes. How was he supposed to eat his dinner with everything all mixed up together?His brows furrowed. How the hell had they figured out his timeline, already? The men and women he'd been watching weren't smart enough to have figured out anything. *Not yet.*

But that Fed . . . the shrink . . . the movie star's boyfriend. He frowned. He was the one who figured out about the keys. Was it possible he was also the one who'd noticed the dates *on which the murders had happened? Was he the one who'd realized they were a Fibonacci sequence? Damn it all to hell. How smart* was *this dude?*

He felt the first trickle of fear run down his spine. Could the guy be smarter than him? Was that even possible? NO! No one was smarter than he was. He was a genius. Dad said so.

He stared down at his ruined dinner, mind racing a mile a minute. And then he smiled. So. Mr. FBI Dude. You think you're so smart. Well, have I got a game for you.

"Agent Page," Tolliver said, hurrying into the conference room. "LAPD just notified us they have a stabbing victim near the Nuart Theatre."

"Are we sure it's one of his?" Page asked, his eyes flicking to the clock on the wall. It was barely eight a.m. They'd purposely come in early in case the perpetrator struck again.

"Yeah," Tolliver said. "The ME called me personally."

"And?" Page prompted. There was something Tolliver wasn't saying.

"And he left a message for you painted in blood on the vic's belly."

For a minute, the room was silent.

"Rhodes, I want you working the crime scene with me." Page said abruptly, moving toward the door. "Smith, Talafiero, Romano, eyes open. He's more than likely going to be in the crowd, somewhere, watching us. And make sure you get pictures of everyone who's there."

Damn it! He would have preferred leaving Rhodes here working his analytical magic safely away from the press. But he didn't have any choice in the matter. He needed Rhodes at the scene.

. . .

"What can you tell us?" Page asked the petite African American medical examiner as Rhodes crouched down beside her, pulling on the powder blue gloves he'd been handed, shoes already encased in booties, completely focused on what he was seeing, oblivious to the yelling reporters *or* their cameras.

"Jerry Lenovo, twenty-three, worked mornings right here at the coffee shop," she said, indicating the building over her shoulder. "Single stab wound to the kidneys. I'm May LaGrange. Just go with May. No need for introductions on your part, Dr. Rhodes, I know who you are, and you're Thomas Page," she added.

Rhodes leaned in slightly as May turned the victim's head and said, "See here? These marks on his neck are consistent with strangulation. I'm guessing a rip cord, or something like that." May lifted one of the victim's bagged hands. "No defensive wounds either that I can see, so he was probably stabbed first, then strangled."

"What makes you think that?" Gia asked, keeping her eyes on the reporters who kept trying to edge forward, but listening intently.

"The man was about two hundred twenty, two hundred thirty pounds. Maybe six two or three. So, unless your perp is a big tall, physically impressive guy, he should have fought back," she answered. "But a stab to the kidneys would have incapacitated him. Brought him to ground."

"Well, that answers that."

"Was anything taken?" Page asked, eyes sweeping the growing crowd, before he looked back at May.

"Got his wallet right here. Still had thirty-two dollars and a credit card in it, along with a grad student ID from Southern Cal. His keys were still in the lock when the second barista showed up and found him. The only thing missing, as far as we can tell, is the key to his bicycle lock."

Rhodes rocked back on his heels, a frown on his face, which Wes picked up on immediately. Something the coroner had said had pinged in Rhodes's brain.

"Got something?" he asked, quietly.

"I'm not sure. Just . . ." He shook his head. But there was something about universities whispering at the back of his head.

"What about the note?" Page asked.

May wrinkled up her nose. Then carefully pulled up the man's' T-shirt while murmuring, "No need to desecrate the dead."

Painted across Lenovo's stomach were the words: "The Golden Rule . . . Ha! Ha! Ha!"

"The Golden Rule—what's that about?" Gia asked, as Page maneuvered the SUV through the crowd of reporters who'd spilled out into the street as if they were going to run after it.

"Do unto others as you would have them do unto you," Romano answered.

"I know the religious context," she shot back, smacking his arm, "but in this case, how does it make any sense, unless the perpetrator wants us to stab, shoot, and bludgeon *him* to death once we find him?"

"Yeah, somehow I doubt that was what he was getting at. Not with the 'ha, ha, ha' tacked on to the end."

"So, like, do unto others as you please?"

"That's what I'm thinking." Romano nudged Rhodes's arm and said, "Hey, Fount, your phone's ringing."

"What?" Rhodes looked around, startled. He'd been staring out the window, mumbling quietly to himself. Something the team had gotten used to when he was thinking.

"Your phone," Romano repeated, "It's ringing."

"Oh!" Fumbling it out of his pocket, he hit answer and said, "Um, yes? Fountain Rhodes here."

And glancing in the rearview mirror, Page saw the lines of concentration fade from Rhodes's face, and he backed off the gas a little.

"What?" Wes asked, noticing the slowing of the SUV.

"Molly," Page said quietly, jerking his head toward the back seat. And glancing back, Wes said, "Ah," in understanding.

"Hey," Molly said softly.

"Hey, yourself," Fountain answered quietly, closing his eyes and sinking deeper into the seat. Letting her voice wrap itself around him, soothing the tension from his body.

"Rough day already?" Molly asked softly.

"Yeah." He couldn't help the sigh that escaped.

"I guess the press conference didn't help things any."

"I didn't see it."

"That's probably just as well. It was not Hollywood at its finest."

"I heard."

"I'm sorry."

"It's not your fault."

"Yes," she said, sighing, "it is. After all, if you'd been dating let's say, a sexy hairdresser instead of me, it never would have happened."

What?!

"Romano *told* you about that?!"

Molly laughed. "Of course he did, and trust me, you do *not* want me messing with your hair. Unless, of course, I'm running my fingers through it," she added slyly.

"Molly! I'm in a car with the rest of the team!"

She laughed. "Not sorry."

"I'm just glad I wasn't driving."

"Page lets you drive?"

"Um. No."

"Yeah, I didn't think so."

"Rhodes," Page said in warning, they were almost back at the station.

"I heard," Molly said, before he could tell her. "Text me later. Love you."

"The Golden Rule . . ." Rhodes paced restlessly back and forth across the conference room talking to himself. "The Golden *Rule?* The *Golden* Rule . . . The Golden . . . something."

"What we need is a name," Wes said, sighing, pushing away a pile of papers he'd been going through.

"Okay," Rhodes said suddenly. Which made the whole team look up at him.

"You've got something?"

"Yes. A fact," Fountain said, nodding. "A single fact we haven't paid attention to yet."

"And that is?" Gia asked.

"The Fibonacci sequence."

"The math connection," Wes said, understanding immediately.

"Yes, we even profiled that he might be a math major."

"All right, we've got our work cut out for us then. We need to contact the heads of every Math department in the area and get a list of all their declared math majors," Page said briskly.

"No, we don't!" Rhodes said suddenly, wheeling round and staring at the white board, suddenly realizing what had been bothering him. "We just need to look at students at CalTech, UCLA, and Southern Cal."

"Why just those three?" Gia asked.

"Because Professor Stone was killed at CalTech, and Donna Young and Jerry Lenovo were grad students—"

"At UCLA and Southern Cal, respectively," Romano finished for him.

"Yes!"

"Well that should make our lives easier," Gia said.

"Okay, contrary to popular belief, we have a bucket load. Who knew math was so popular?" Romano said a short time later, shaking his head. Beside him, Gia snorted. When he looked up, she jerked her head toward Rhodes, who was staring at him, an annoyed look on his face.

"What? Oh! Sorry, Fount, forgot you're one of those math nerds," he said, grinning. "Any ideas how to narrow these down?"

"Yeah, I do actually. I think we should start with anyone who dropped out recently."

"Okay, we're looking at . . . six," Gia muttered. "Cross referencing their names with owners of late model, light-colored American sedans now. And that would leave us with . . . three.

"Okay that's weird—they each went to one of our target schools." Running her finger down her computer screen, she added, "No priors on any of them. Brewster was a grad student. He's a middle school teacher in Pasadena. Lester is working at the zoo—go figure—and . . . Drake doesn't seem to be working anywhere. Looking at driver's license pictures now, and . . . he's who I'm going with. Not only because he's the one who went to CalTech, but because Jordan Lester is African American, and Malcolm Brewster is listed as six foot five, blond with blue eyes, while Drake is listed as five foot eight, with brown hair and hazel eyes.

"Romano, take Talafiero and do a low-key drive by Drake's house. Pick a neighbor or two to talk to, unless he's out mowing his yard."

"Excuse me, Detective?" Sully poked his head into the room. "We've got another one. Lupe Suarez, an elementary school teacher. She didn't show up for work, and since she always called in if she was going to be late, the school got worried. When the uniform who went to talk to the principal found out she always stopped for coffee at the same place, he called it in. We found her about ten minutes ago at a coffee shop about three blocks from here."

"Asshole's taunting us," Tolliver snarled.

While Fountain said, "One, one. There won't be any more bodies today."

"According to his neighbors, Drake's lived in the house with his dad for the last sixteen years," Romano said when they got back an hour later. "No one could remember what the story on the mom was, but she never lived there, and his dad died in a freak accident about six months ago. He fell off a ladder and smashed his head open."

"And there's the trigger," Rhodes said quietly, writing on the board. "His kills started right about then."

"What else did you find out?" Page asked.

"He was home schooled, so none of the local kids ever got to know him. He didn't play sports. He was always a loner with his nose in a book."

"Dad worked at home. A researcher of some sort, although no one knew what he was working on," Romano added.

"How to raise a psychopath?" Rhodes suggested.

Wes grinned. Now that was pretty funny.

"And Drake senior owned a late-model compact white Ford," Talafiero added.

"Let's get an APB out, and Tolliver, we need a warrant for the house, now," Page told him.

"There is not a damn thing here that's telling me anything," Romano said as they went through the house for the second time.

The house was a small white stucco ranch, typical of the area, with terracotta tiles on the roof and a carport that leaned slightly to the north. Its age showed in every nook and cranny. Romano thought it was at least fifty years old. He thought the shag carpeting probably was too, judging by the shape it was in. The kitchen still had the original avocado appliances—that were probably worth a fortune now. It was like being in a time warp. Right down to the ugly brown-plaid furniture in the living room.

The house itself was meticulous—almost as if no one lived in it anymore—with that slightly stale air feel to it. Like the owner was away on vacation.

Or had another lair.

He could feel the short hairs on the back of his neck prickling. Like they were being watched—but that was ridiculous. They'd found no evidence of security cameras, inside or outside of the house.

Just two beds, neatly made. Two closets with clothes hanging in them—two footprints. Even though Drake's father had been dead for six months now. It gave him chills. Who kept a dead person's things, as if they still expected them to walk into the house and take back up their life where they'd left it?

"Oh, I don't know," Fountain said. He was staring at some old circus posters that had been framed and hung in a row down the living room wall. "Don't theses seem out of place to you? Why would a twenty-four-year-old man have posters from the circus on his walls?" he asked, rocking back on his heels as he studied them.

"Because something happened at a circus he went to once, maybe?" Wes answered, pulling out his phone, fingers flying on the keypad as he entered something into the search engine. "And we have a winner. Sixteen years ago, a trapeze artist was killed during a performance at the Staples Center."

"Do you have any details of the injuries that killed him?" Rhodes asked.

"Let me ... Ah, his head was smashed in."

"Bingo," Fountain said softly.

"A hundred to one Drake was sitting in the vicinity," Romano said.

"And then six months ago, he sees his father smash open *his* head—a psychotic explosion," Gia concluded.

"Uh, guys? I just found out what Drake senior was researching all these years . . ." Rhodes called out, having moved on from his perusal of the posters to their flanking bookcases. He was flipping through the pages of an old notebook he'd pulled out of one of them. "And as it turns out, I hit the nail on the head."

Which got everyone's attention.

"It looks like Dad knew Drake was a psychopath, and he spent his life studying him. There are literally hundreds of notebooks here filled with his observations, going all the way back to when Drake first started out—tasing animals" Fountain added.

"Looks like he hasn't lost his taste for that kind of thrill yet, either," Gia said, showing them the taser she'd found in one of the bedrooms.

"I think we're done here," Page said quietly.

EIGHTEEN

HA! HA! HA!

So they knew who he was now. Not that it mattered. They didn't know where he lived. Really *lived. They'd found Dad's house, but he wasn't there. As for his place? Yeah, good luck to them, finding it. He snickered to himself as he watched the Feds moving about. Poking and prying into things they shouldn't. He had a clear view of what they were doing, seeing as how he was right next door. Dad had bought the house using a fake name, back when things like that had been easy to do. Set up a whole identity of a nice widow with a small inheritance. Hadn't wanted any nosy neighbors peering in at them, seeing as how it had been close enough to have a lovely view right into their family room.*

He pulled off his wig and fake boobs and tossed them onto the coffee table, then pulled off his old lady boots and wiggled his toes. He was exhausted, and it wasn't even eleven yet. Still, he'd been prepared for it. Had a loaded, breakfast strata he'd made last night all ready to be heated up. His mouth practically watered at the thought of the rich gooey cheese, sharp onions, and salty bacon and ham he'd put in the egg mixture. Maybe he'd even pop the top off a cold one. Hell, he'd earned it with two kills in one day, and beer went with everything, right? Even breakfast.

Two kills back to back. He grinned. Oh yeah! The big dude had been especially exciting. The little Mexican chick not so much, although she had struggled a bit. He wondered if the Feds had even found her yet.

He picked up the keys he'd taken, studied them. The dude's bike key was interesting. It looked like a long narrow tube. The chicks was one of those novelty keys: an apple with the initials of the local elementary school on it. They'd look good in his collection.

He stretched and dragged a hand across his face. Ugh, the makeup had begun to itch. How the hell did chicks wear this shit all day? Time to shower and get it off and think about tomorrow a little bit. He needed to decide if he was going hunting as Granny Big Boobs again, or as himself.

And he needed to get his ass across town. There was a certain movie star's brother he needed to check out.

"Uh, Detective Tolliver?" Sully said, opening the conference room door and coming in. "We have a problem. We've got eyewitnesses from both of today's murders who describe the person last seen with the victims as an older woman, with, um, big boobs and gray hair."

Tolliver frowned as Rhodes murmured, "That's not the first time a witness saw one of the victims with an old lady."

"Yeah, the owners of the mom-and-pop shop saw Donna Young leave with one," Talafiero said, reaching for the stack of witness statements.

"Which means, what? He's dressing as an old lady for some of his kills?" Tolliver rubbed his eyes and muttered, *damn*, then said, "Explains how he's getting close to some of them. Who thinks Norman Bates when they're chatting with Granny?"

"There's something else too, sir," Sully added. "Lenovo wasn't the only one with a note. He left one for Dr. Rhodes tucked into the waistband of Miss Suarez's skirt." And stepping forward, he handed Rhodes an evidence bag, inside of which was a small note card.

"Dr. Rhodes," Fountain read out loud, "I'm flattered you came to L.A. personally. I recognized you this morning in the alley. I liked the way you were so thorough. Did you get my play on words yet? Rumor has it you're a genius. Me too. I wonder which one of us is smarter. Well, I guess we'll find out tomorrow. I do hope, for your sake, that you figure out the appointed place and time in our little game by then.

Yours sincerely,

Mark Drake."

Shaking his head, Romano said, "So he *was* watching us in the crowd, then slipped away while we were there to kill Miss

Suarez. Guy's got balls." Which earned him a sharp look from Tolliver.

"Gia, we need those crowd photographs." Page said darkly. "He'll be in them somewhere."

"On it," she said, head already bent over her phone as she uploaded them to her laptop.

"Wouldn't that be, *she'll* be in there somewhere?" Rhodes asked.

"Technically speaking," Wes agreed, as Gia started sending the crowd scene images to the fifty-inch flat screen that hung on the wall beside the white boards.

Page nodded. "We're looking for anyone with gray hair. Regardless of how old they seem," he answered, staring intensely at the first few images. "Let's get those isolated first, then we can whittle it down from there."

"I think . . . yeah, I think this might be him here," Gia murmured, fingers flying on her keyboard as she made a copy of one particular image, enlarged it, then sent it to the screen so they could all see it.

"That is definitely a granny with gray hair and big boobs," Romano concurred.

"I'm not seeing any other gray-haired women in the crowd, of any age," Wes added.

Scanning the photographs one last time, Page nodded. "I'm not seeing anyone else, either. Anyone?"

A chorus of softly murmured noes and nopes answered him.

"All right, let's make a copy of that," Page ordered. As Gia sent the image to the printer in the corner, he added, "Detective, we need verification from the witnesses that that's who they saw."

"I can do that now," Sully said, before Tolliver could answer. "They're both still here." And, taking the photocopy from Gia, he was out the door in a flash. He was back only a few minutes later. "Positive ID from both of them."

"Excellent," Tolliver said with relish.

"All right," Page said, "Let's get moving with this. Gia, send a copy over to our local Bureau office. We need them to run a simulation of what that woman would look like as a man. This gets priority over anything else they're working on, unless it's a possible terrorist attack. If they give you any flack, call Assistant Director Franklin. If their simulation matches Mark Drake, then I want side-by-side pictures of him as both a man and a woman on the evening news. Someone knows him. As for the rest of us, we need to concentrate on what these notes mean."

Across the room, Rhodes cleaned off a white board then wrote:

The Golden Rule

Ha! Ha! Ha!

A play on words

The appointed place at the appointed time.

"And that's it in a nutshell," Romano murmured.

"Looks like gibberish to me, except for that time and place thing," Sully said, staring at the words. "Like he's expecting you to know what that means."

"If he follows his pattern, it means the time and location of tomorrow's kill," Page told him.

"And the how of it," Wes added.

Roxy nodded. "If he sticks to his pattern, the how is by hitting someone over the head."

"While the time will be around lunch time," Romano added. "In a grocery store parking lot."

"So all we need to do now is figure out which one," Sully said.

"A play on words," Fountain muttered softly, ignoring the conversation going on behind him as he studied the white boards with their grisly pictures and notes pinned beside them. A play on words. So, what did you do if you were playing with the meaning of words? Or the order of words? Or the letters *in* the words? He titled his head. No, not a cryptogram. A word jumble then? Or—and suddenly he got it.

"It's literally a play *on* words!" he half shouted, startling the room into silence behind him as he grabbed up a marker and started drawing lines on a map of L.A., dividing it into sections that had meaning only to him.

"Got something, Fount?" Wes asked, his voice calm, a rock in the maelstrom of thought surging through Fountain's brain, anchoring him to the here and now before he got carried away.

"Yes!" Fountain said, spinning around to face him. "It's not *the* Golden Rule, it's *a* golden rule. A golden *spy-rule!* That was the 'play on words.' God, I'm so stupid!"

"Care to explain that to the rest of the class?" Romano asked.

"He meant the *golden spiral*."

"Not getting any clearer," Romano said.

"It's a type of logarithmic spiral where the distances between the turnings increase in a geometric progression," Rhodes said distractedly, looking back at the map again. There was something . . . something not quite right.

"Well that explains *everything!*"

"A play on words . . ." He bit his lip, scrunching his eyebrows together. What was he missing? "If it's a play on words, that means it's not a golden spiral exactly—" His eyes drifted across the white boards and landed on the one with the dates of the murders. "It's not a golden spiral because he used a Fibonacci sequence!"

"Clear as mud," he heard Romano murmur.

"And although you can *plot* a spiral using a Fibonacci sequence, it isn't a true logarithmic spiral . . ." His voice trailed off, so where was this going?

"Rhodes? In English?" Romano requested.

Rhodes flapped an annoyed hand at him. He was thinking,

damn it. "That was English." He all but snapped as a stared at the geometric sequence he'd loosely drawn on the map.

"If you say so," Romano said, sharing an amused look with Talafiero.

"The Golden Rule. Ha! Ha! Ha! What do you mean if you say ha, ha, ha?" Rhodes asked suddenly, turning to face everyone, again.

"You're making fun of someone or something?" Gia answered, staring at him like he was an idiot.

"Making fun of something," Rhodes repeated. "Making fun . . ." His eyes widened as everything fell into place. "You're making fun of the fact that if you plot a spiral using a Fibonacci sequence, it's not round!" he said suddenly.

"Again, care to explain to the rest of the class?" Romano asked.

"Both the Fibonacci and golden spirals look like . . . like a conch shell, or a hurricane with a long tail," he explained, hurriedly. "But a *logarithmic* spiral is tight and round."

"Like the *eye* of a hurricane," Wes said in understanding.

"And where the eye is, is the location of his next kill," Page finished for him.

"Exactly!" Rhodes exclaimed, and using a different colored marker he drew a circle starting at West Hollywood, curving around to Santa Monica, then back up to West Hollywood before curling his circle around into a hurricane's eye.

"Fount, that's the most lopsided circle I've ever seen, and it puts the eye of your hurricane in the middle of a golf course," Gia pointed out.

Fountain bit his lower lip, chewing on it as he stared at the map. She had a point, but he knew he was right about this. So what was wrong?

"What if we include the kill site in Hollywood," he murmured, "then the eye of our hurricane would be, here—" Taking yet another color of marker, he drew a larger circle, starting in Hollywood, curling down to Santa Monica then up and around back to Hollywood, before curving down to end with the eye at the Staples Center. "That doesn't make any sense either," he huffed.

"Unless it's subconscious on his part," Wes pointed out.

Tolliver nodded. "Makes sense to me, since you said this whole thing started with the death of a trapeze artist at the Staples Center back when he was a kid. And there are a bunch of convenience and grocery stores in the area. It'll be easy to blanket the area with plain clothes officers," Tolliver said with a great deal of satisfaction.

"I don't think we'll have to. He's not going to attack anyone where there are any surveillance cameras, so that should whittle down the number of possible locations considerably."

"What difference would that make? We know what he looks like now, more or less," Sully asked.

"You're right, except I think he probably scouted out his next kill site a while ago, and it won't occur to him to change it now."

Fountain shook his head. "There's something still not quite

right—something I'm missing." Something that was bothering him about the whole thing. The Staples Center location didn't feel right . . . "I don't think that's where he's planning to be," he added, turning back to the map with the crime scene locations on it, which killed the conversation going on around him.

"It makes sense to me," Tolliver repeated.

"But it leaves out some of the other crime scenes," Roxy said, nodding.

"What if you add the crime scene in Pasadena?" Wes asked, trying to picture a hurricane that included it, but failing miserably.

"I don't think so. That was personal. Like that family. They don't fit into any part of his equation."

"So, what's wrong with his next kill being near the Staples Center?" Tolliver asked.

"It's too obvious," Fountain murmured. Which won him an incredulous look from the man.

"You think it's maybe the play on words thing again? Like he wants you thinking hurricane while it's really something else?" Romano asked.

"Or it could be a part of the game," Gia suggested.

Suggestions flew fast and furious, bombarding him, until Fountain could feel a headache coming on. The kind that threatened to shred his brain.

Then Page put a stop to it.

"Let's take a break, step away for a little bit, grab a late lunch, let things percolate," he stated.

"Seriously? You're going to go out to lunch right in the middle of this?" Tolliver asked.

"Yes." Page told him. "We need to step back and let our subconscious minds sort things out. Staying here going around in circles isn't going to get us anywhere."

"Hey." Molly's voice was like balm to Fountain's soul.

Getting up and moving away from where the rest of the team sat, the debris from their lunch scattered around them as they worked their way through various desserts, Fountain said, "Hey, yourself."

"I heard about the new murders. You okay?"

He sighed. "Frustrated. I feel like there's this thing just right —there, and I can't quite grab on to it."

"You will," she said confidently. "So, this weird thing happened to Michael this morning during his office hours."

"Yeah? How weird?"

"Weird enough he decided to come home right after."

Which made Fountain stop pacing. "What happened?"

"This kid came into his office and asked if he was going to be taking over Professor Stone's classes. When he said no, the kid said, 'aw, bummer.' Then, as he was walking out, he paused in the doorway and asked Michael if he was my brother."

"What did this kid look like, Moll?" he asked, a tendril of fear sliding between his shoulder blades.

"Hang on, Michael's right here. I'll put him on speaker."

"Michael, what did this guy look like?" Fountain asked urgently. Across the room, Wes looked up and met his eyes, as if he sensed something wasn't right.

"He was just kind of average. Brown hair, maybe brown eyes?"

And suddenly, Fountain flashed back to the feeling that someone had been watching him when he'd been with Molly. Or, more likely, watching her.

"Molly, I need you to think very carefully. Have you seen anyone who matches that description lately?"

"No, I haven't been anywhere—*wait!* The waiter at the Soul Garden Café the other day! He had brown hair and eyes, and he was really attentive, now I think of it. Sort of hovering."

"The Soul Garden Café?" Fountain repeated carefully.

"Yes," Molly answered faintly. "Does that mean something to you?"

"Yeah, it does," he answered. One of Drakes earlier kills had been in the alley behind it.

He took a slow, deep breath, then very calmly said, "Molly, I need you and Michael to get out of the house right now, get away from L.A. for a few days. And take Jonathon with you," he added. "Like, *right now*. Just throw some things in a bag and get out of there."

"Fount, why? You're scaring me."

"Good. Pack now and go. Call me in five minutes and tell me you're on your way to somewhere else." Then something else occurred to him. "And get Ricki out of the city too." Because she'd been there, lit up plain as day in the parking area in front of Molly's house when that guy had jogged by. She'd been at the café, too. And this being Hollywood, it wouldn't be hard for him to find out who she was, if that had been the man they were looking for.

"What's wrong?" Wes asked, as Fountain hurried back to their table.

"He was in Michael's office not long after his second kill today, asking if he was Molly's brother."

"What?"

"And I think it's my fault."

"How could it be—" Gia started, but Fountain cut her off.

"Because I think he's been following us. Her. I thought there was someone the other night outside the restaurant watching us when we arrived, and then later, there was this guy jogging by her house when we got there. But then when she told me about Professor Stone missing a key, I forgot about it. And now she's just told me that her waiter the other day at the Soul Garden Café was a little too attentive."

"The Soul Garden Café?" Page and Wes said together, concern evident on both their faces.

"Yeah."

"Shit," Romano said softly. "So this guy, he keys in on Fountain and Molly at the Academy Awards and decides he wants to play a game with the FBI. He's probably thinking someone from the local office is going to be running the investigation, then he sees Fountain is here, thanks to the media coverage, and gets to thinking how much more fun it would be if he made his game personal.

"So he starts watching Molly," Gia said nodding. "Studying her routines. Looking for a time and place he could take her."

"But just to cover his bets, he takes a look at her brother," Page agreed. "I think he probably went to his office this morning so he'd know what Michael looked like."

"And that's what that part of today's note meant." Wes said thoughtfully. "'I hope you figure it out for your sake.' He's planning on going after one of them."

"Which is why I'm having her, and everyone close to her, leave town. Not that Molly would be easy to take. Her schedule is all over the place, and her driver is also her bodyguard. But Michael would be a sitting duck. As a professor, his schedule is pretty much set in stone."

"Where are they now—Molly and Michael?" Page asked, pushing back his chair.

Fountain checked his watch. "Two minutes from being in a car heading out of town, along with their housekeeper. And hopefully her manager is right behind them."

"Good."

What the hell? he thought, as the counter guy turned up the sound on the TV in the corner to ear-splitting levels. The dude's mouth fell open at whatever it was he was seeing.

All he'd wanted was some peace and quiet with his lunch, a moment to chill, which was why he'd come in later. But nooooo. Damn well better be someone shot the president, he thought, turning to look, then froze. The slice of pizza in his hand forgotten as a photograph of Granny Big Boobs stared back at him. A second later, his mind caught up with the words the reporter was saying.

"The FBI says this woman, pictured here, is a person of interest in connection with the string of murders from Santa Monica to Pasadena they believe are the work of a serial killer. If you know this woman, please call the number at the bottom of the screen."

For just a second, panic overwhelmed him before his brain kicked in. Okay, so they had a picture of Granny Big Boobs, big deal. They had no idea who she was, and he doubted any of his senile neighbors would make the connection. All old people looked like her. Still, he'd miss the old girl. Fucking Feds. Good thing he had his drag queen persona all ready and waiting to go out and get a little action. Huh, could be fun. Throw a few dead gay guys into the mix, shake things up a bit. But not until after tomorrow. He took a big bite out of his pizza and nearly choked on it as another picture went up on the TV.

"They are also looking for this man in connection to the killings. He's described as being around five foot ten inches, one hundred and fifty pounds with brown hair and either brown or hazel eyes."

"Oh, like that's helpful," the counter guy snickered. "Shit, that pretty much covers both me and you, dude," he told him. "And all my

friends." And just like that, his heart stopped trying to claw its way out of his chest. The guy had a point. The picture was crap.

Until the pictures went up on the screen again, this time side by side.

Shit, if any of his neighbors saw those like that, they might make the connection, and he felt the rage starting to build inside him. The Feds thought they were so clever, did they? Thought they had him cornered? Well, the joke was on them. They wanted to play games with him? Well, good luck with that, because he was about to change the rules.

NINETEEN

THE GAMES PEOPLE PLAY

Huh, the redhead was back, pacing up and down the driveway, phone pressed to her ear. Left hand gesturing wildly. Damn it, he hadn't been expecting anyone else beside the movie star to be there. He slowed and looked around, then made the decision to pull into the driveway anyway. A reconnaissance expedition with no one the wiser, and the redheaded chick as his cover. Perfect.

She paused her conversation as he pulled up beside her and rolled down the window. "What?" she barked, before he could say, "excuse me?"

"I'm trying to find"—he paused, lifting the courier envelope up as if to read it—"a Dr. Fine?"

She huffed out a breath and impatiently waved farther north. "Third drive up that way." Like she knew where the nonexistent Dr. Fine lived. Then, turning away, she continued her phone conversation saying, "Look, Martin, she'll be back later. Just come here say, around seven-thirty? We'll do dinner." Pause. Then, "No, I have no idea where she went. She said she had to go somewhere with Michael. She wanted me to go with her, but like, no? I'm busy. I can't just go rushing off during the day." She opened her car door, got in, but before she closed it said, "Okay, see you then. Seven-thirty, bring a bottle of wine or something. She won't be happy to see you."

Well, damn it, he thought, turning around then heading north up the road like he really had something to deliver. He chose another driveway, pulled in, waited a minute, and fumed.

So, the movie star had left for the day and taken her stupid brother with her. What was with that? He paused midfume and considered the thought that the FBI had figured his next move out. But, nah, they couldn't have. No, the stupid woman had simply messed up his plans by default. She was the most unpredictable person—which was why he'd gone and taken a look at her brother to begin with. It always paid to have a plan B. Though now it looked like he needed a plan C too, since her brother had gone with her, wherever it was they were going.

He gave an annoyed growl, then pulled back out onto the winding road and found himself directly behind the redhead, then followed her from the movie star's house to her gated office. Nothing else to do, since neither the movie star nor her brother would be back until later. Though, from the sound of it, he wouldn't be able to get close to either one of them—not tonight anyway . . . And he didn't want to wait until tomorrow.

But the redhead, now. He knew who she was, the movie star's manager, and she'd do in a pinch. Getting out of his rented Prius, he prowled the office's perimeter, looking for a way in. But there were too many cameras, too many people coming and going. He'd have to get her someplace else. Someplace less crowded. Sooner or later, an opportunity would present itself. All he had to be was patient.

Turned out, he didn't need to wait that long before she was back outside, climbing into her Tesla. How very earth conscious of her. He snickered.

He followed her to her gym, where she parked next to a friend's car and went in with him. An hour and a half later, they walked back out together. Then he followed her out to Glendale—seriously? Glendale? To the parking lot of a grocery store where she found a slot right by the entrance in plain sight of a camera.

Keeping one eye on her car, he started a search of the internet, trying to find out more about her. Okay, so he'd already known she was the movie star's manager, but no matter how many different things he tried, he couldn't find out where she lived. So much for getting to her place ahead of her—he'd just have to follow her home. And then, he smiled, and then he'd see how smart Dr. Fountain Rhodes really was.

"Fount, I can't reach Ricki." Molly's voice was one part tired and one part worried. The tired part, he knew, was the crash after the adrenaline rush from fleeing the city. The worried part caught his attention.

"She was supposed to be leaving the city with you."

"She refused. Said she had things to do and that they were

too important to cancel, but now she's not answering her phone. It's going straight to voicemail."

"When did you last talk to her?" he asked, the first faint touch of unease sliding across his shoulders.

"Right before we left. She pulled into the drive just as we were locking up the house. That's when I tried to get her to come with us, but she was all, 'Can't you leave later? We need to have a meeting,' and I was like, 'No, we're going now, and you need to come with us,' which is when she said she was too busy and that we'd just get together later.

"It wasn't until we got to Catalina that it occurred to me that she thought we were just going to be out for the day, so that's when I tried to call her the first time. But she's still not picking up, Fount, and it's been hours."

"Moll, do you know where she was going after she left the house?"

"She said she had some errands to run, then she was going to the gym and the grocery store, and probably home after that? She should be there now, Fount. I mean, it's almost six-thirty."

"Give me her address, and we'll have a squad car go check on her."

"Problem?" Wes asked when Fountain hung up, watching his partner staring at the piece of paper he held on which he'd just jotted a note.

"Molly can't reach her manager."

"I thought she was leaving the city with Molly."

"Yeah, I did too."

"Damn, and now she can't reach her?"

"No," Fountain answered. "She was at the house when Molly left, then she was going to run some errands and go home, but she doesn't seem to be there, and Molly's worried about it. I'm going to ask Glendale PD to run a wellness check."

"Her phone probably ran out of juice, and she hasn't plugged it in to recharge yet," Gia offered. "Happens all the time."

Yeah, it did, Fountain thought, but not to someone like Ricki . . .

"Agent Rhodes, this just arrived for you," a uniform said, coming into the conference room a short time later and handing him a special delivery envelope.

"Were you expecting something?" Page asked, eyeing the familiar square envelope.

"Um, no." And then very carefully, he set it down on the table and pulled on a pair of latex gloves before reaching for the envelope again.

A familiar note card slid out into his hand. A twin to the one that had been found on Lupe Suarez.

"Dr. Rhodes, I just wanted to let you know that I'm kind of pissed off with you right now. Really? Plastering those crappy, pictures of me all over the place. Definitely not part of the game, so guess what? Since you changed the rules, I'm going to change them too. But I'm not completely unreasonable, so here's a little hint. I really hope you figure it out.

Look at her with her skinny blue jeans,
Damn she's a looker with her bright red curls
Always had a thing for little bitty things
Gonna make her mine tonight,
Or die trying.

Well, I guess we'll find out soon enough. I'll be so disappointed if you can't.

Yours sincerely,

Mark Drake

"What the hell is that?" Tolliver exclaimed.

"The lyrics to *Die Trying*. A song by Broken Wing off their multiplatinum-selling album, *Screw Love Anyhow*," Rhodes said, without batting an eye.

"Wait. You listen to Broken Wing?" Gia asked, grinning.

"Yeah. Why wouldn't I ? I listen to lots of things. And their lead guitarist is a friend of my brother's. That's where Molly went, to his place on Catalina Island."

"Seriously?" Gia, Roxy, and Romano said simultaneously, as

Wes added the lyrics to a white board, hiding a smile of his own. His partner was full of surprises.

"So, what do the lyrics mean? If they mean anything." Tolliver cut in.

Sully opened the conference room door and said, "Agent Rhodes, Glendale PD couldn't find anyone at the address you requested a wellness search for. Her car is there, so they had the apartment manager open the door. No sign of her. No sign of a disturbance."

For a minute, the room was silent before Fountain very quietly answered Tolliver.

"They mean he's changed his MO. He's made the game personal for me. He's taken Molly's manager. Ricki—Erica O'Brien. The song suits her perfectly. She's tiny, has red curls, and Molly can't reach her."

"Which is why you requested the wellness check," Tolliver said in understanding. "By taken, you mean he kidnapped her?" he asked, exchanging looks with Sully.

Page nodded. "If the lyrics are really a hint, then it would seem so."

"Do you think the rest of the lyrics mean anything?" Sully asked, gesturing at them.

"More than likely."

"So, he has something planned for tonight . . . instead of tomorrow," Tolliver said, frowning at the white board.

"Death by cop," Wes said, grimly. "If we find him."

"I think so, yes," Page agreed.

"And if we don't find him?" Sully asked.

"He'll kill her."

"Then we need to figure out where he's taking her," Sully said. "Are there any other hints in this song?"

"That's the question," Romano said, his fingers flying over his keyboard. "And with any luck, here's the answer. The next verse says:

Gonna drive her out to the country tonight,
  So the stars are like diamonds all around her
  Make sure there's only her and me around
  When I get down on my knees and ask her
  Plan on loving her for the rest of our lives
  And beyond, into the hereafter.

"So, he's taking her out of the city someplace?" Gia suggested.

"Somewhere remote," Romano added.

"Shit," Tolliver swore softly, then turning to Sully, he said, "Make sure the highway patrol has the information on his vehicle and that they know he's most likely kidnapped Ms. O'Brien and is headed out of the city with her."

"I'm not so sure about that," Wes said, frowning. "His comfort zone, for the most part, has been between here and Santa Monica."

"But there's no countryside between here and there," Gia

pointed out.

"No, but there are parks," Romano said.

Backing up so he could see all the white boards, Fountain murmured, "He likes to play games. Complex, twisted games using logic and logarithms and . . . words!" He twisted around and grabbed the letter Drake had left for them that morning. "Did you get my play on words?" he read out loud. "A play on words . . . He likes to play games . . . word games . . ." He paused, staring at the white board, his brows drawn up tightly. "No, not a hurricane!" he suddenly exclaimed. "A galaxy!"

"Uh, Rhodes? Hurricanes and galaxies aren't exactly the same thing," Romano pointed out.

"No, they're not! It's another one of his word games!"

"Explain?"

"They're both, incorrectly, used sometimes as examples of logarithmic spirals, and there's a perfect place you can see the stars in L.A. besides going out to the country."

"An observatory," Wes said, nodding.

"Exactly! And," Fountain added, turning back to the map of L.A., "if I draw our hurricane like this—starting in Santa Monica, then adding in the crime scenes in Century City, Beverly Hills and West Hollywood, then go around to Pasadena where Professor Stone was killed, and down to clip the Staples Center, the natural curve will pass through the crime scene in Hollywood, ending with the eye at—"

"Griffith Park Observatory," Wes said nodding. "So the song was another word game since not only is the observatory where you can see about a thousand stars, but it's about as close to being out in the country as you can get without leaving the city."

"Not to mention it's closed today making it the perfect place to play out his end game!"

"How the hell would you know it's closed on Mondays?" Tolliver asked.

"I did my undergrad at CalTech," Fountain answered. Which earned him an appraising look.

"Now we know the place, we need to work on the time," Page said, satisfaction lacing his voice.

"Um," Fountain hesitated.

"You have an idea?" Page asked him.

"Yes. It's pretty farfetched, but the Eta Aquariids meteor shower should be visible from just after midnight until dawn there."

"The what?" Tolliver asked, but Page cut off Rhodes before he could get started.

"It's not important. All that is, is that now we know the 'when', too. Which doesn't give us much time to get into place. Roxy, notify the SWAT team and let's figure out a rendezvous point someplace where he can't see we're coming."

"I don't think that's going to happen, Page," Romano said, pulling up an aerial view of Griffith Park. "If he's up there already, he pretty much has a bird's eye view of the entire city."

Sweeping his eyes across the picture, Page nodded. "Then we go in boldly."

TWENTY

THE OBSERVATORY

He watched them come, headlights gleaming, as they made the long drive across the park then fanned out across the parking lot. There were so many of them. He puffed his chest out with importance. Of course there were, how else could they hope to stop him? And they had arrived with minutes to spare. Dr. Rhodes had proved to be a worthy adversary.

He wondered if he would be brave, too. Courage was such a nebulous thing. One could talk about it a great deal, but when push came to shove . . . he grinned. Well only time would tell, and he doubted very much that the good doctor had figured out what was really going to happen here.

The opening bars to Broken Wing's hit, "When Time Stood

Still" rang out suddenly in the silent confines of the SUV. Molly's ring tone. *Shit.*

Fumbling to drag his phone out of his pocket, Fountain started a stuttering apology when his eyes met Pages in the rearview mirror.

"Answer it." Page told him quietly.

Incase something else has happened—the unspoken words hung between them.

"Molly?"

"Fount, she just called me. Ricki," Molly said, relief and tears seeping through her voice. "She was with her boyfriend and had her phone turned off."

"Wait. Ricki's all right?" At his words, Page looked sharply at him.

"Yes, but Martin's missing."

Fountain blinked. "Wait. Martin Riley's missing?" What the heck?

"Yes! Ricki was supposed to meet him up at the house at 7:30. They've been trying to talk me into co-staring in another movie with him. This was a last ditch attempt only Ricki didn't realize I wasn't going to be there and now Martin isn't there either."

"Okay, back up a minute, and I'm putting you on speaker so Page can hear. Now, what makes her think Martin's missing?"

He heard Molly take a deep breath before she answered. "Because, when she got to the house his car was there and the driver's side door was open, but he wasn't in it. His cell phone was on the ground, but the keys and Martin were both missing. She got scared, tore out of there and called the police. When they couldn't find him, either, they called in more people to do a sweep of the house and grounds and he's not there, Fount. He's not anywhere."

At the mention of the missing keys Fountain and Page exchanged a look.

"Molly, are the police still there?"

"Ye—yes. I have Officer Conway on Michael's phone."

"Give him my number, I need to talk to him, now."

A few seconds later Rhodes's phone vibrated with an incoming call.

"Fountain Rhodes," he said briskly.

"Max Conway," The officer responded.

Niceties out of the way, Fountain quickly directed the officer to where the computer was that the houses surveillance cameras sent their images.

"Martin Riley is six foot two. He wouldn't have been easily overcome. But the fact he's missing could be tied into a case we're working on."

"The serial killer," Conway said knowingly.

"Yes, and since our suspect is only five foot nine or ten, with any luck the cameras caught whatever happened."

"Okay, running through to our time slot and, here comes Riley. He's getting out of his car," there was a pause, then the officer said, "and you're not going to believe this. But someone tasered Riley from off camera."

And Fountain couldn't help the little shiver that went through him.

"I don't get it," Tolliver said shaking his head. "He sent us a note, specifically suggesting he was going to kidnap Erica O'Brien. What if he was just trying to get us off track with that? What if Martin Riley was his intended victim all along? Wouldn't that mean that we could also be wrong about where he's taken him?" he asked, squinting across the parking lot to where the Observatory gleamed whitely in its flood lights.

"I don't think we're wrong about any of it." Page answered. "I think he sent us the note fully intending to take her. He knew she was going to be at Molly's around seven-thirty and staked out the place. But when Riley showed up first, he took him instead."

"Lovely," Tolliver muttered. "As soon as the press finds out, they're going to be all over us."

"Not if we move first. Lieutenant Boyton, are you're men ready?" Page asked the SWAT team leader.

"Locked and loaded, and my guy is slipping through the scrub around back right now. He should be at the base of the building just about the same time as we get to the stairwells."

"All right. Everyone know what they're doing?" Page asked. And at the murmurs of assent he said. "Then let's go, and no heroics," he added, looking at Fountain.

They moved quickly across the brightly lit parking lot, trying to keep out of the floodlit areas as much as possible. Grotesque shadows danced in front of them as they slipped from light to dark and back again, the observatory hulking like a medieval fortress in front of them. The central rotunda looming over the rest of the building, dark and forbidding. The Halls of the Sky and Eye stood sentinel at either end, telescopes shuttered beneath their domes.

Ramps and stairwells linked the rooftops and terraces that ran from one end of the structure to the other. A seemingly single storied building. But that was a lie. There was a second story, below ground on the front side, but on the backside, where the ground sloped steeply down, the second story was clearly visible, the rotunda rising above it like an impenetrable tower.

And somewhere out in the scrubland around it, a solitary sniper made his way toward the shadow cloaked east side near the planetarium, his sights set on the stairwell that led up to the east side terrace. From there he could slip across to the elevator shaft and up onto the roof of the central rotunda, giving him a clear view across the observatory's rooftops.

. . .

"The suspect is on the rooftop over the Hall of the Sky," a voice said through their earpieces moments later.

"Copy that," Boyton replied before turning to his second. "Harper take your men up the east staircase. I want half of you on the east observation terrace and the rest on the roof over the Hall of the Eye."

Then turning to Page he said, "The rest of us are going to split up as follows: Jorgen's going to take the rest of my men up the staircase to the west terrace, while I'll lead your team up the stairway that goes to the roof over the Hall of the Eye. Questions?" He glanced around, but when there were none said, "On my mark then," and with a drop of his hand, half of his men slid off to the left while the rest of them, with the Federal agents in their midst, broke away to the right.

Moving cautiously now, hearts pumping adrenaline as they crept up the staircase on the outside of the building, they slowed perceptibly at the last bend until only Page and Rhodes were still moving forward. At the top of the stairway Page broke to the left, Rhodes to the right only to stop dead. Across the rooftop Drake stood grinning right in front of them, a knife held tightly to Martin Riley's neck. Blood beading up around it.

"Hello, Dr. Rhodes," he said teeth bared in the semblance of a smile.

"Drake," Rhodes answered, then looking into Riley's panic-struck eyes said, "Hello Martin," his voice calm, soothing, as if nothing out of the ordinary was happening.

"Drake," Page barked, "let him go."

Drake shook his head, his grin widening. "No, I don't think so . . . he's my bargaining chip."

"What is it you want?" Page asked, his voice cold, clipped.

"First . . . I want you off the roof. All of you, both here and over there." He jerked his head toward the Hall of the Sky. "Then I want the rest of you off both terraces. What? You didn't think I'd notice them? Don't be ridiculous, Agent Page. I know the Observatory like the back of my hand. The only person who stays is Dr. Rhodes."

"No."

Drakes eyes darkened. "It's not negotiable." And very slowly he deepened the cut on Riley's neck, the stuttering sobs that had been leaking out of him, turning into a gasping wail as the blade sunk in. "I'm sure Dr. Rhodes can tell you, if I cut much deeper, Riley will bleed out before you can rescue him. Now get off the roof, Agent Page! You have until the count of three. One, two—" he laughed as Page dove for the stairs as he started to say three.

"And now it's just us, Dr. Rhodes. Just the way I planned it. You won't be needing that," he added, nodding at the gun in Rhodes's hand. "But you already knew that."

Slowly Rhodes set the gun down on the ledge beside him.

"Let him go," Fountain said quietly. "You don't want him."

"No, I don't." Drake agreed, looking quickly out at the

parking lot below them. His smile deepened. He could see the men walking slowly back toward their vehicles. Faces peering anxiously up toward the rooftop where he stood.

Nine, ten, eleven, twelve plus five Federal agents. All accounted for.

"Okay then, what is it you really want?"

"You, Dr. Rhodes. It's always been you," Drake said simply.

"He's going to kill you!" Riley choked out, frantically.

"No. He won't," Rhodes told him with quiet certainty. "A dead FBI agent will only get him cut down in a hail of bullets. A live one will get him anything he wants."

"No," Martin tried to shake his head, then gasped as the knife dug deeper. "He's got a gun. He's going to shoot you."

Rhodes glanced down and saw the butt of—something—in Drake's waist band and couldn't quite help the jerk his heart made.

"It's not a gun," he said quietly. "It's a taser."

"Very good." Drake purred. "Now why don't you tell our little Martin here all about tasers, Dr. Rhodes?" Then he made a little giggle and said, "Oh but how silly of me, he already knows!"

"Hurts," Riley gasped out. "Hurts so bad." And a tear leaked out of the corner of his eye.

"How sweet. Concern for your rival. He is your rival, isn't he?" Drake chuckled. "Although I'm afraid you seem to be striking out on that account, Martin. Our lovely Molly Whittier seems quite—taken—with the good doctor." He grinned at

Fountain. "Not that I think you need to worry much about Martin stealing her away from you. He's not very smart. Took him *forever* to figure out I was their waiter the other day when he and the redhead—Ricki whatshername—were extolling the virtues of some movie they want Molly to make with him." He shook his head. "Funny how no one ever notices the help. They say all kinds of things in front of us they shouldn't. Molly was so very proud of you, though, for figuring out about the keys. But, enough about that.

"Tell me, Martin. What makes you think our dear doctor won't just turn and walk away. Leave you to me? He can't like you very much, sniffing and snuffling around his girlfriend constantly."

"Not—not his rival." Martin managed to gasp out. "I make *movies* with Molly."

"Tsk, tsk. Shame on you Mr. Riley. I've been watching you and you paw her every chance you get. But, that's neither here nor there. I'm relatively certain that Dr. Rhodes is going to upstage you once again. You see, while you play the hero on the movie screen, he's going to play the part right here, in all its tawdry reality. Swapping himself for you, so you can crawl off into the sunset. Or whatever it is the vanquished do. Isn't that right, Dr. Rhodes?"

"No!" Riley whispered hoarsely. "He isn't really going to let me go and he's going to kill you! He's got a gun. I saw it." He insisted, swaying just a little bit on his feet. Drake tightened his hold on Riley's throat, making him cough and choke as he fought to breathe.

"Let him go," Rhodes said urgently.

And Drake laughed. "See, Riley. He's simply *dying* to upstage you, isn't that right, Dr. Rhodes? Even though you know what replacing him is going to cost you. Don't be shy, now, I know you know. You've been tasered before during FBI training and the pain you felt then when your muscles seized up and you couldn't breathe is replaying through your mind, even as we speak. You know exactly the agony you're going to suffer. Because Martin is absolutely correct. I am going to shoot you, just not with a gun. Where would the fun be in that?"

"Noooo. He's going to kill you! He's going to taser you over and over until—"

"Martin, listen to me!" Rhodes said urgently, cutting the hysterical man off. "That's *not* how a taser works! It *cannot* discharge continuously. It works by passing a short burst of current through the muscles making them suddenly contract. The second the burst ends the muscles relax and the pain is over just like that. You know this. It's what happened to you. At the very worst, the one he's got will discharge in a thirty second burst. And yes, it's going to hurt, and I will probably scream when it hits me, but it *cannot* kill me. And that's all that matters."

"Such the hero," Drake said, laughing delightedly.

. . .

"Page, we need to get a guy up there now," Wes said urgently. "I'm with Riley on this. Drake hasn't gone through all the trouble of getting his hands on Rhodes just to taser him. He's got something else planned."

"I've got a man almost there," the SWAT team commander said softly. "He's just at the edge of the building. If your agent can keep the subject engaged just a few minutes longer, he should be able to make it undetected up onto the roof of the elevator."

"Rhodes," Page said urgently into Fountains earpiece, "you need to keep Drake talking. We need another two—three minutes to get a line on him."

"So, despite your pretty speech, we both know what's going to happen, Dr. Rhodes." Drake said smiling. "And now, to make sure you feel the full effect of my little toy when it hits you, you're going to take off that vest you're wearing."

"No." Rhodes said, shaking his head.

"No? Then I'm going to slit his *throat!*" Drake yelled pressing the knife in even harder.

"No!" Rhodes cried out at Martin's muffled scream of terror. "No! Okay, I'll do it."

"What? The sight of blood makes you squeamish, does it?" Drake said, amused. "The vest, Dr. Rhodes. I'm losing patience . . . Ah, much better."

. . .

"Captain, is your man in place yet?" Page demanded.

"He's working his way across the rooftop now."

"Tell him he's cleared to shoot as soon as he can see the target."

"Any last words for your rival, Dr. Rhodes, before I set him free?" Drake teased.

"Martin, listen to me. No matter what you hear, you run straight down those stairs. And you keep right on running until you reach someone whose vest says FBI on it. Got that?"

And with tears running down his face Martin Riley whispered, "I'm sorry."

"There's nothing to be sorry for," Fountain said, stealing himself as best he could for what was coming.

"Kiss, kiss, mwah, mwah. Oh wait. Speaking of kisses, did you remember to kiss your Molly goodbye, Dr. Rhodes? Yes? Good. Then I think we're done. Ready? Then—*run, Riley, run!*" Drake yelled laughing uproariously, as he drew his taser and pointed it at Rhodes, as Martin disappeared down the stairway.

And Fountain screamed—as he charged Drake. The unexpected sound, coming before it should have, throwing the man's aim off when he pulled the taser's trigger. The barbs rattled harmlessly past Rhodes, as he slammed Drake to the ground. But the man was fast. Wicked fast and white-hot pain tore across Fountain's shoulder as Drakes knife slashed across it, an enraged snarl twisting his face.

Twisting and scrabbling frantically, Fountain pushed him away, and across the dark, a flash of light lit up the night sky and the man who was Mark Drake jerked once. Then twice.

Did they really think it was going to end so easily? He thought, as his face twisted into a leering grin of pain and malice. Did they really think he was going to let his prize get away? Staggering to his feet, Drake pulled his gun from its hiding place in the back of his pants and pointed it at Fountain. That idiot, Riley, hadn't been wrong. No one in their right mind only brought a knife to a gunfight. And he wasn't an idiot. He was brilliant. He was—

A third flash of light lit the night, and as Mark Drake fell forward, his finger tightened on the trigger.

TWENTY-ONE

END GAME

Dad? Dad! He couldn't feel his limbs. Couldn't see. Couldn't breathe. Was he sick? Was h— nooooo! They'd shot him. The bastards. They'd killed him. But they hadn't won. He had. He'd taken their precious Dr. Rhodes with him.

Looking up into the brilliant night sky, Mark Drake smiled. The stars really were like diamonds, he thought. And then he thought nothing at all.

Wes stood peering up through the brightly lit night. Up on the rooftop he could just see Rhodes's tall, slender frame. He couldn't see Mark Drake at all. Beside him he could hear Page murmuring into his wrist mic, he hoped Rhodes was listening to whatever it was that Page was saying.

And then his partner screamed and vanished from sight

and Wes was running even as a flash of blue and a muffled bang cut through the night. Martin Riley came flying out of the stairwell, tears streaming down his face. He heard Page yell, "Gia get him—" as he ran past him, Page not a half step behind. A second bang cut through the air, then a third. They took the stairs three at a time, afraid of what they would find.

Just let him be alive, just let him—Wes cleared the stairs and saw his partner's crumpled figure on the ground, Mark Drake splayed out beside him.

"Rhodes! *Fountain!*" He called out, clearing the distance between them in seconds. Automatically kicking the gun out of Drake's hand, he fell down on his knees beside Fountain.

"Officer down!" Page yelled into the mic on his sleeve. "We need a medic, *now!*"

Frantically Wes began searching for a pulse.

A quiet cough, a mumbled, "Mmmm 'kay," as his partner opened his eyes and stared blearily up at him.

"Sure you are," Wes agreed, relief coursing through him, but he could feel the trembling that shook Rhodes's body beneath his hand.

Another cough, and the jerking of limbs as Rhodes tried to sit up.

"Hey! You're not going anywhere yet, Fount," Wes said gently, pushing him back down as the medic appeared and crouched down across from him. "Not 'til you get an all clear!"

"'M fine," he protested, weakly.

"Rhodes." Page's stern voice stilled him. He closed his eyes, then opened them again suddenly, struggling to rise as his mind kicked back into gear.

"*Riley!*"

"He's fine. Now quit moving," Wes gently admonished.

"Drake?"

"Dead."

Rhodes closed his eyes, quiet for a moment before he said, "I was wrong."

"About what?"

Rhodes opened his eyes and looked up into the bemused expression on his partner's face. Behind Wes he could see the other members of his team crowding around, checking on him for themselves.

"I should have known he'd have the taser with him. That he had more than one charge for it."

"There wasn't any way for you to know that!" Gia exclaimed.

Rhodes shook his head, wishing the medic would be done already. He was fine, except for the fact that he couldn't stop shaking. He coughed again wishing the guy would stop fussing already.

"I should have known." He repeated.

"How?" Romano asked, clearly humoring him.

"It's what I would have done."

Romano blinked. Then grinned.

"Really," he protested weakly. "If I was as sick as he was, I would have wanted to inflict pain, play with my victim before I killed him and what better way than with a taser? That's not the only thing I got wrong."

"No?" Gia asked curiously, kneeling down beside Wes, and taking Fountain's hand in hers.

"The profile," Rhodes answered simply. "I missed the most crucial part of it."

"That he was a paranoid narcissist." Page said, sighing.

"I should have recognized the signs," Rhodes persisted.

"You weren't the only one who missed it," Page said firmly.

"What difference does it make?" asked Tolliver having made it up onto the roof just in time to hear Fountain berating himself.

"It placed Rhodes in unacceptable danger."

Tolliver shook his head, confused.

"Paranoid narcissists are convinced they're omnipotent," Page explained. "When they're challenged by a person they think is of equal or greater intelligence they tend to fly into a rage and lash out at that person. Drake saw Rhodes as a threat to his superiority. That's what set this all-in motion," he added, gesturing around him. "By deviating from his set pattern and taking a hostage—one who Rhodes knew personally—Drake was able to manipulate a situation where he knew he could get his rival alone and punish him."

"And it worked," added Romano, "up to a point."

Tolliver raised his eyebrows and Romano smirked. "Like most people, he underestimated Rhodes. Nice scream by the way," he added, grinning.

Tolliver raised his eyebrows in surprise. "That wasn't real?"

"Why would I scream?" Rhodes asked puzzled.

Tolliver floundered for an answer. "I—you—but you *did* scream!" he said finally. "You even told the movie star you'd probably scream."

"As a distraction," Rhodes agreed, completely misunderstanding what Tolliver had been implying. "In order to give SWAT a chance to do their job, I needed Drake to be completely focused on me. The taser was an unforeseen complication. So I screamed."

"That was good work," Page said quietly. "And now it looks like your ride's here," he added as a second medic appeared with a gurney.

"Page I'm fine, it's just a scratch, I don't need—"

"Romano, you and Wes finish up here, I'll ride with Rhodes." Page told them, ignoring Rhodes's protests. "You can meet us at the hospital when you're through."

"Page—"

"Hey, Fountain?" Wes said, patting Rhodes's shoulder. "Not a fight you're going to win. You're going to the hospital. End of story, we'll see you there."

"Wait!" Fountain called out suddenly. "What time is it?"

Wes and Page exchanged a look. "Twelve-fifteen a.m.," Page answered.

"Good," Fountain mumbled. "He stuck to the Fibonacci sequence right to the very end." And Wes couldn't help it, he burst out laughing.

. . .

Page stayed with Rhodes until they were ready to clean and sew up his wound. Then stepping outside, he took a deep lungful of the warm California night air and speed dialed the 9th number on his phone.

"He's all right," he said immediately, when the call was answered. "He has a minor stab wound through the meaty part of his shoulder that's being seen to right now. They'll probably insist he stays over night, but he really is all right."

A quiet sob, a steadying deep breath.

"Thank you," came the husky voice. "Oh god, Page, when I saw it was your number—"

"He's going to be fine, Molly. I just didn't want you finding out about it from one of the paparazzi."

"And Martin?" Molly asked, fearfully.

"Shook up, but not hurt."

A little sob reached his ears, then, "Where are you?"

"Cedars Sinai."

"Can I come?"

"I think that would probably be a good idea. I'm going to put him on medical leave for a week, and it's not going to go over well with him."

There was a pause.

"How about two weeks?" She countered.

Page couldn't quite stop the smile that twitched his lips. "I think that could be arranged." He agreed.

"Excellent" And Page was relatively certain he heard a little purr in her husky voice.

"Ready?" Molly asked, as they paused looking through the glass doors of the hospital to where a crush of reporters waited outside for them. Eight steps away, Stan waited stoically by the back door of the Town Car ready to whisk them out of there.

Fountain sighed, taking her hand as he gave her a wry smile and said, "Ready as I'm going to be."

And with a little laugh, Molly pressed a fleeting kiss to the corner of his mouth before pushing him through the doors in the mandatory wheelchair and out onto the sidewalk, where they were nearly blinded by the sudden onslaught of camera lights flashing in their faces.

"Dr. Rhodes, Dr. Rhodes, are you all right?"

"Were you shot?"

"Did you shoot anybody?"

Voices shouted.

The last question made Fountain blink and for the barest instant he thought he saw a fleeting grin flash across Stan's face as their eyes met. He definitely heard the little snuffle snort of laughter Molly made and when he glanced at her she rolled her eyes, her back safely to the cameras, so no one saw her.

Pausing, at the open door of the limo, Molly gave his fingers a quick encouraging squeeze before he stood up and turned to face the paparazzi. With a little smile in place he looked across at them and said, "I'm fine, thank you for asking." Then turning back to Molly, he helped her into the limo, and climbed in after her, giving a huge sigh of relief when Stan closed the door shutting out the rising cacophony of inane questions they'd started shouting at him again.

"Did I shoot anybody?" he asked indignantly. "Really?"

And with another little squeeze of her fingers Molly said, "Well, this is Hollywood and the only thing they know about the FBI is what they see in the movies."

They had a quiet dinner at her house on the beach, with Jonathan hovering anxiously around him. Not completely convinced he wasn't hurt worse than he was until Fountain beat Michael in a noisy game of Mario Kart, and then was beaten in return amid a great deal of shouted insults, cat calls, and ridiculous preening by the victor.

As they wished each other good night a short time later, Michael said, "Glad you're okay, Fountain. You scared the crap out of us for a short time there. I would not want your job, chasing down the bad guys at all. But thank you for what you do."

Which made Fountain squirm just a little. "I don't usually," he said. "Chase down the bad guys, that is, except on paper."

"Any way you have to do it man, makes the world a little safer for the rest of us to live in."

.   .   .

And later still, as he stood out on the deck with Molly, watching the waves roll in, she said, "I'm really glad to know you don't usually chase the bad guys like that. God, Fount, I was so scared for you."

Drawing her close with his good arm, and resting his cheek against her hair he whispered, "I was scared, too."

They stood like that for a little bit, taking comfort in each other's arms before Molly said, "So, I was thinking. Since Page has given you two weeks mandatory medical leave, that maybe we'd take that trip to Tahiti I promised you?"

For a long moment Fountain didn't answer. Being alone with Molly on a tropical island had a certain appeal. Long, lazy, uninterrupted days to do nothing but make love to her. And yet there was something else he'd rather do. Something he'd been thinking about for a while now.

Pulling back just enough to see her face, heart racing just a little, he said, "You know what I'd really like to do? I'd just like to go home to Arlington with you. And then maybe, after a few days, we could go see your Mom. And then after a few days with her, I thought we could go see my Mom and Dad too."

He heard her breath catch in her throat as she looked up at him, eyes wide as she realized what he was implying. And then suddenly she giggled and buried her face in his chest, which wasn't what he'd been expecting.

"Moll?" he asked uncertainly.

"Oh god, I'm going to embarrass myself so badly by going all fangirl when I meet your Dad."

With a laugh of his own in relief and happiness he said, "Well he's going to go all fangirl over you, too. He's a huge fan."

"Don't you mean fanboy?" She asked, eyes alight with laughter as she looked up at him again.

"No. He's going to go all—oh my god, I can't believe I'm meeting you!" Fountain told her, raising his voice into a high-pitched falsetto, that reduced her to more giggles.

"You're such a dork."

"Well, at least he knew who you were when I told him I was dating you. I had to Google you when Page asked me if I knew."

Sliding her fingers into his hair, she said, "And I loved that about you. I loved that you didn't know. That you wanted to be with *me* and not some—grand illusion. That I could just be Molly to your Fountain."

"Always," he told her. Then, "Come home with me, Molly."

For the barest heartbeat her eyes searched his, before a radiant smile lit up her face and he thought he could see the beginning of forever in her eyes as she said, "I would love to go home with you, Fountain Rhodes, and I would love to meet your family."

This book was a long time in coming and is dedicated to:
My Friday morning knitting friends—Joy, Tracy, Beth, Stacy, Nicole,
Linda, and Cindy who helped me figure out the 'kissy' bits

To my writerly friends—Babs and W.M. who share table space with
me at the best coffee shop on the planet and kept me putting words on
the page—even if it was really slowly

And to my sib, Andrea Sickler, for hearing about this book every
morning for the past year and then going above and beyond by
waging war on all those errant commas and scenes that just wouldn't
behave for me—could not have done this without you!. So many
hugs.

And, as always, to my guys. Love you so much.

Special thanks to Maddie Farlow at Clause & Effect for friendship
and patience above and beyond when everything came to a grinding

halt, and, of course, for all things editorial and for the amazing cover! Could not do this without your magic touch.

And to Danielle Romanetti for allowing Fountain and Molly to visit her real-life shop, Fibre Space.

ABOUT THE AUTHOR

Hilary lives in North Carolina with her husband, who, sadly, does not want to talk about interesting ways to murder anyone. Her two grown sons, however, don't mind indulging their mom. A well-known knitting designer, best known for her enormous 'house cozy' shawls and hilarious MKALs (which you can find on her Ravelry knitting group Criminal Knits), she got into writing knitting mysteries because she felt the genre needed a little spicing up with some really hot guys, their zany girlfriends and a good dose of all knitterly things from an insiders perspective.

To Contact Hilary:
Criminalknits@gmail.com

ALSO BY HILARY LATIMER

Knitting Game Mystery Books:

Malice in Wonderland – Book 1

The Dyeds of March – Book 2 (coming March 2020)

Dancing in the Dark: An FBI Knitting Game Mystery Spinoff – Book 1

Pattern Books:

Happy Hour

As The Heel Turns

A Midsummer Knit's Dream

A Dark and Stormy Knit

THE KNITTING GAME

The Knitting Game is an online MKAL hosted by the author every few years on her Ravelry Group, Criminal Knits. The Traveling Scarf, featured in her book *Malice in Wonderland,* was a previous game that ran for 42 weeks . . .Yes, the author is insane.

Patterns connected to this book:

Dancing in the Dark – available through the author's Ravelry store

Patterns are available in my Hilary Latimer shop on Ravelry.

RAVELRY GROUP

CRIMINAL KNITS
for the serial knitter in all of us

Made in the
USA
Columbia, SC

79906295R00159